Storm's Warning

by

Ryan Jo Summers

Winds of Destiny, Book Two

Storm's Warning

Cover Art by *Najla Mahis*

The Wild Rose Press, Inc.
PO Box 708
Adams Basin, NY 14410-0708
Visit us at www.thewildrosepress.com

Publishing History
First Edition, 2024
Trade Paperback ISBN 978-1-5092-5662-4
Digital ISBN 978-1-5092-5663-1

Winds of Destiny, Book Two
Published in the United States of America

Dedication

Storm's Warning is dedicated to all those who chase their dreams. Storm Gallagher is a free spirit who lives life on her terms--bold and fearless. She finally meets her match in Brody McGee. To anyone who dreamed of embracing life fearlessly, strap in and hold on tight as Storm and Brody take you on a wild ride. My hope for all my dear readers is that they get to embrace life with the same passion and zeal Storm does. Spending time with Storm as I wrote this taught me a lot about how life should be lived.

Also, this is dedicated to the excellent team at The Wild Rose Press. Storm's story is book two in a series that means so much to me. I am honored they allow me to share the Sweetwater Harbor stories with my readers.

Praise for Ryan Jo Summers

Chapter One

Storm Gallagher knew they were following her, the two men about fifty feet behind. Clean shaven, short hair, and average in appearance, they looked like regular travelers. One wore a blue striped shirt, navy sport jacket, and tan khakis. The other guy wore a white shirt, khakis, and a black blazer. They blended in with the business crowd coming off the Atlanta flight, but she would bet anything as to why they were on her tail. She had not noticed them during her first flight, but they most certainly were following her. Maybe she picked them up at her last connection bringing her here to Atlanta, Georgia.

Regardless of where they found her, or when, she needed to ditch them, and quick. She had worked too hard to gather this data, just to let two goons steal it now. If they thought she was simply going to hand it over like a lollypop to bullies on the playground, they were in for a surprise.

The overhead speaker din announcing arrivals and departures beat a tattoo in her mind as she considered her options. Lighted signs for gates and flight information and restaurants flashed all around her. What she needed was a distraction, a way to throw them off her backside, slip off to her gate, and quietly make the last leg of her journey. Once she made it home, she would be safe, along with her important data.

People moved around her, traveling alone or in pairs or groups. They laughed, skipped, rushed, shuffled, and rolled, dragging a wide assortment of luggage. There were plenty to choose from to aid in her diversion.

Storm looked around the groups and clusters of people as she slowly made her way to gate B-6. She spotted a man walking out of the restroom and moving toward the water fountain. She glanced at his ring finger, noting it was bare. She looked around for anyone obviously waiting for him. He appeared to be traveling alone. She smiled at her perfect luck. He would do nicely.

She reached into her carry-on bag, curled her fingers around something, and approached the brown-haired man as he exited the restroom and moved to the drinking fountain.

Touching his shoulder, she whispered at his ear, "Play along with me. There's twenty bucks in it for you." Flinging herself against the wall by the fountain, she took him along, pressing her lips to his mouth and brushing her body against his.

She felt his stiffened shock and saw his brown eyes widen, but he did not back away. She reached down and captured his hands, placing them around her waist. She slowly inched one of his hands to her hip, near her butt, and laced her other hand through his thick, wavy hair. A shiver sliced over him, and she smiled at the reaction. Bolts of startled energy passed between Storm and the man she held.

He stood rigid, barely breathing. He kept the connection between their lips but without fully engaging.

She cast one eye on the pursuing duo. She watched them pass by, looking around at the other passengers. They barely gave the passionately kissing couple by the drinking fountain a second glance.

Finally, with the goons far enough ahead, she released him, licking her lips. Whatever gum he had been chewing tasted good, fruity, though she suspected he had now swallowed it. Pushing him away, she pressed a paper bill into his palm. "Thanks. Loosen up a little, though." She tossed him a satisfied smile and sauntered away, her red carry-on swinging against her hip.

****

Standing there, his lips moist and his heart racing, Brody McGee stared after the redhead, utterly flabbergasted. Had she really blown by like that? Once she disappeared into the crowd, he looked down at the crumpled twenty-dollar bill in his hand. The money was proof she had.

What the devil just happened?

Well, whatever it was, it had passed like a midnight storm. A midnight electrical storm with wavy red hair, skin-tight black jeans, and a white sweater. He huffed a breath. That woman, whoever she was, was a serious complication, a major trouble. Right now, he didn't need either one. All he wanted to do was complete this wretched trip and collect his friend. He had to convince Calder to come to his senses and return to the real world. Then the two of them could get back as fast as possible.

Delightful, surprising, and wet kisses from wild redheads with full lips was something he had no time for, despite how powerful and delicious they might happen to be. He had work to do. He shouldered his bag, pocketed the twenty-dollar bill, and headed for gate B-6.

He was one of the last ones to the gate, most of the other passengers having already boarded. He glanced out the window and noticed this plane was much smaller than the jet he had flown in on from Atlanta. To his shock and horror, he saw only a single propeller mounted in the front, already spinning. Looking toward the wings, he failed to see any engines. Could the thing stay aloft? He huffed another breath and wondered what he was getting into.

Showing his pass, he boarded, exchanging brief pleasantries with the crew. Only two attendants and two pilots. A much smaller crew, he realized. Well, it was a shorter flight, to go along with the smaller plane. His heartbeat skipped up to an uneven rhythm, making him dizzy. Oh, Calder Finn owed him big time for this. He absolutely hated to fly. And the sight of this plane was more than disconcerting. His pulse raced at the horrors his mind imagined as he stooped slightly to enter the aisle.

He quickly did the math; two seats per side of the aisle, that was four seats per row, and he quickly counted twelve rows. The plane had a maximum capacity of forty-eight passengers. He was in seat 7B.

He found his seat, glanced at his seatmate, and felt his heart skip a beat. He could not believe his luck. Happily settled in the adjacent seat at 7A was none other than the wild redhead. Swallowing, he wished he still had that last stick of gum. But she made him swallow it in complete shock when she accosted him. "So, we meet again." He pushed his carry-on bag into the overhead compartment and slid next to her. "I do believe we've met before."

She looked up from the magazine she'd been flipping through and gave him a coy smile. "I do seem to faintly recall seeing you somewhere," she hedged. "Was it near a drinking fountain?"

Minx, she wanted to play games. "Yes, I believe it was." He fastened his seat belt and drew in a shallow breath.

The attendants closed the doors, and the plane roared to life with a backward lurch.

His stomach dropped. Between the rumble of the plane, and knowing they were soon to be airborne, compounded by the redhead beside him, he wondered if he might have a heart seizure before he reached Calder's town.

Brody closed his eyes and concentrated on the din of the passengers around him. Laughter, whispers, and various snippets of conversation filled his ears. Unfortunately, with his eyes shut, he also homed in on the steady breathing of the woman next to him. He peeked over. "Why the money?"

She shrugged, lifting her shoulder absently.

He noticed she seemed completely at ease with the plane.

"You looked like you could use it. I needed your services. Fair trade?"

He ran that through his mind, finding it more insulting than complimenting. His heart bounced unevenly, and hot bile clawed through his throat. He searched for the airsick bag and cursed his partner next to him.

The redhead withdrew a nail file and began filing

her left fingernails.

Distraction. He needed something to distract him from his air sickness. "Why did you need my services?"

"Wasn't it enough? Do you want more?"

"No." He shook his head. Was she saying his kiss was worth more? Or that he looked like he needed more money? Brassy woman. She was entirely too intriguing. He had no time for crazy women. Listening to her now, though, he could not help but run his tongue over his lips, tasting the sweet fruit of her lip gloss. A faint pattern of freckles splayed over her tanned face. Beneath her tan was a dewy pale complexion. His fingers remembered the softness of her skin, like a fresh rose petal. She felt fit and athletic when she pressed her warm body against his. She kissed like a woman who knew what she demanded from life.

He needed to get away as soon as possible. The plane roared, and he felt the liftoff as the tarmac gave way to grass and treetops. His stomach rolled, and he felt faint. His heart pounded, and blood roared in his ears.

The redhead switched hands. Then she set the file aside and looked at him. She extended her hand. "Storm Gallagher."

Taken aback by her sudden move, Brody paused. Slowly reaching for her hand, he was not overly surprised by her strength. "Brody McGee," he supplied. "What kind of name is Storm?"

She pulled her hand back and sniffed. "It's my name."

He hadn't meant it unkindly. On the contrary, it fit her perfectly. Not only did he feel like a storm had just ripped by, but she did also remind him of a miniature tornado of energy. That red hair, streaked with blonde, hanging in loose waves and green-blue eyes were a combination that could upset a man's soul. Looking closer, he noticed the thin braid along the sides, ending in a pair of green beads. What did those braids feel like? Had she been christened Storm at birth, or was it a nickname? Had she been a pint-sized whirlwind as a child?

Surprised at his thoughts, he hastily reeled them in, turning away.

The attendant came by, offering bottles of water.

Thankfully, he reached out, needing a cold one. Silence filled their space for a while as the plane coasted along. Brody found the silence between them pleasant, though electricity still charged the air. Even in an airplane, he wasn't immune to her beauty and energy. Like him, she seemed to have other things on her mind. They stared out the window, where he could not help but notice her profile.

Brody had to admit, Storm's calm nonchalance about flying went a long way to soothe his nerves. He watched her swallow the last of her water and considered saying something about helping to ease his fear of flying.

"Can I give you a lift once we land?" Storm asked, after she replaced the cap on her empty bottle. "My car is in parking."

"You don't even know where I am going." His ears popped as the plane descended, and he shuddered.

She rolled her eyes and tucked the bottle into the seat pocket. "It's not that hard to figure out. There's a chance you might be catching another flight to go farther up or down the coast, but I kind of doubt it. So considering I'm going almost to the farthest point away, it's safe to assume you are probably going to somewhere between where we're landing and to where I'm going." Again, she shrugged. "Hence, the offer for a lift."

He smiled. "What if I am going where you're going?" His partner had said he was at the farthest town before you hit either ocean or Virginia. The thought made him wince internally.

"Sweetwater Harbor isn't that big of a town. If that's where you're going, you can rent a mule."

She was kidding, right? She had to be kidding. What had Calder gotten him into?

The wheels came out, and the plane began its descent in earnest.

He barely noticed it this time. "We're complete strangers," he pointed out. "You don't even know who I am, what I am capable of."

"Not so much complete strangers," she said, slicing him a sideways grin. "We've kissed already."

The grin rooted him to his seat, white heat spiraling through him. The brassy minx still wanted to play games. Suddenly the idea of sharing a car with her sounded like an excessively big temptation. He calculated it would be almost a two-hour car ride once they landed. Two hours in a car with her could be time well spent.

No, on second thought, he wanted his own transportation. He just might have to bodily throw Calder into the car and escape out of town. He'd better play it safe and rent a car as he had planned. He needed to stick to the plan, no distractions. Or attractions. This crazy redhead was making him forget his plan. "No thanks. I'll just run the risk of having the only other car in town beside yours."

"Suit yourself."

He moved back, allowing her to go before him.

Shouldering her bag, she spun around, another wicked grin on her lips. "Thanks for the help back there," she whispered.

Before he knew it, he felt her drop another wet kiss on his lips.

"See you around, Brody McGee."

His lips sizzled, and he slowly ran his tongue over them, tasting her fruity flavor. "My God, woman! Where have you come from?"

"Oklahoma," she tossed over her shoulder, amusement lighting her blue-green eyes. Laughing, she exited the plane.

It took Brody a minute, and the passengers pushing behind him, to realize he was still standing like a dolt, watching her go. He blinked, her rich laughter trailing behind her and teasing him like exotic perfume.

****

After checking over her shoulder numerous times, halting, and backtracking, Storm was convinced the goons were no longer on her tail. And neither was the handsome man from the airplane. Brody Mc-something-or-another. She was relieved about the goons but felt a stab of disappointment about Brody. She would have liked to spend a bit more time with him. For entertainment's sake, of course.

Suddenly eager to get home, she shrugged off the memories of Mr. Tall, Dark, and Handsome and rushed out to long-term parking. She could almost feel the salt air from here. The air was so vastly different here in

North Carolina than the fierce storms she had been surrounded by in Kansas and Oklahoma. Looking up, shielding her eyes from the sun, she scanned the clouds, reading their story. They had so much to tell her. Like an old friend, the North Carolina blue sky and puffy white clouds spoke to her rapidly, as if they were as excited at her arrival as her.

Reaching her shiny blue, mid-sized, four-wheel-drive, off-road SUV, she clicked the fob in her hand, watching the round lights flash. She tossed her twin duffels into the back, slipped in behind the wheel, rolled down the windows, donned her pink-tinted aviator sunglasses, and finally turned the key. The engine turned over with a satisfying purr. Giving one more glance to ensure no one was watching her and finally convinced she was alone, she backed out of the space. No goons and no Mr. Mc-handsome-whoever-he-was. Eagerly, she wanted to get going. She could stop along the way and get some coffee and maybe a sandwich. But right now, home was calling her.

Soon, spinning out of town, along the expressway that yielded to quieter roads, she watched the scenery change. Munching the bistro sandwich she bought at a gas station along the way, she reflected on the circumstances that brought her off the tail end of a long chase and back home. Big sister River was getting married. Wow, who would have ever thought she would marry?

Storm had always worked under the assumption that she and River were of the same mind-set that marriage was just not made for them. River was too busy—or devoted, depending on your point of view she supposed—with Frank Finn and the weight of the town's future to worry about such a burden as marriage.

And as for Storm herself? Well, what man could hope to keep up with her globetrotting and storm-chasing life?

No, if any of the sisters were to marry someday, it would have to fall onto practical Raine's shoulders. And Winter alone had the responsibility to carry on the Gallagher name, once he finished his military traveling and escapades.

Except now River was getting married. Swallowing the last of the sandwich, she pressed harder on the gas pedal. She'd make this two-hour trip in an hour and a half. She could hardly wait to meet this guy. He had to be something special.

Chapter Two

The drawbridge was up when Storm finally reached town. She braked to a stop and rested her arms on the steering wheel, waiting for the boat. She was a little surprised at how much she had missed Sweetwater Harbor. She smiled at the seagulls flying and crying overhead. Even having to wait for the bridge was a welcome sight. For now anyway, give it a little while. Finally crossing over into town, she turned left, towards Raine's bakery. Before she went home, she wanted a visit with her baby sister.

Sweet Obsessions looked just like it had when she was last in town, except with a couple new pictures of master creations framed on the walls. She smiled at her sister's creative talent.

Busy with a customer, Raine glanced over as Storm entered, her face lighting up. "Storm! You made it." She held up one finger. "Wait just a second." Finishing with her customer, she slipped around the counter and swept her into a hug. "So good to see you!"

"You, too, Raine. Hey, the place looks good, and you look great. I love your hair! A shoulder bob fits you perfectly, especially with your dark hair."

"Thank you. I like it, too," Raise agreed as they separated, and she pulled Storm to a pair of high-legged barstools at a tiny table. "Are you hungry?" she asked. "I can get us a torte or pie?"

"Later, Raine. Just sit and talk with me." Storm grabbed her hands, keeping them locked on the table. "Tell me about what's been going on."

Raine slanted a dark eyebrow. "You mean in Sweetwater Harbor or with River and Calder?"

"Calder? Is that the man who is marrying our sister?" She'd forgotten the name of the Finn boy next door. "Oh, the news is all one in the same, so go ahead, tell me everything. First, start with how business is here for you?"

"Business is good. I've been in a profit all year," she continued, explaining about Calder Finn coming to town months ago, the friction between him and River, and the gradual mutual attraction until the fateful day out on the "Wind Quest" where he proposed. The townsfolk were pretty much the same as normal with no new births or deaths to report beyond Frank Finn's terrible passing.

"Yeah, I still can't believe that." Storm shook her head. The Finns had been an institution, always next door.

"The funeral was lovely, though. You should have come."

Storm shook her head. "I couldn't. I was in the middle of this dual supercell system in Kansas and Nebraska. It was just awesome, keeping me busy hopping all over the plains. I barely had time to pee."

"Stormie," Raine said with a sigh. "Always chasing."

"Raine," she countered, with an exaggerated sigh. "Always baking."

Tugging each other's hands, they broke into spurts of laughter. "Good to have you back. How long are you staying for?"

"At least till the wedding. I can't miss that. Afterwards, I don't know. We'll have to wait and see." Long enough for the goons to give up their search and the airports were safe again. Long enough to make sure Calder was going to take good care of their big sister. Long enough to enjoy a visit with her family.

"Anything new and exciting in your world, beyond supercells?"

Storm glanced around before leaning closer. "I have some really phenomenal research from the last several storms. Oh, yeah, and you won't believe this guy I met on the flight in." She exhaled deeply. "He was so hunky."

****

Unbelievable. Brody slowly crossed the drawbridge and drove back somewhere in time. Exactly where in time he wasn't sure, but this place was still back there. He had the sense that time had somehow gotten lost or simply forgotten and never made it to this sandy, desolate outcropping. Why hadn't some hurricane already pulled the whole chunk back into the ocean by now?

And what in the world made Calder Finn, of all people, want to stay here? Sure, he had been raised here. Brody knew that from stories his partner had told him. But to want to stay? What was wrong with him? The only way Calder ever spoke of his hometown was his keen desire to get away and never return. Brody shook his head. He did not understand any of this.

Okay, at least he noticed other cars around, not a mule as that dangerous little redheaded tornado had indicated. So the town had electricity and probably a gas station. Maybe. So where was Calder?

He pulled into the big parking lot of the marina and fished his cell phone out. Dialing his partner's number on the screen, he thumbed it once, watching the call connect. Phone service was a good sign, too, and he breathed a sigh of relief as he counted the ring tones. One…two…three…four…five. Calder always had his phone no more than a foot away. Why the delay? Finally, he picked up just when Brody was convinced he was being sent to voicemail. "Calder, I've just arrived in….town," he faltered a moment, looking around. Town seemed to be such a strong word. "Where are you?"

"Where are you, Brody? I'll come to meet you. It's easier."

"Someplace with lots of boats. Near a lighthouse and a bridge. A marina?"

Calder laughed. "I know that place. Just hang tight. I'll be there in ten minutes or less."

About to ask more, Brody heard the phone go dead in his hand. Puzzled, he closed the call, still looking out at the seagulls and boats. He drew in a lungful of air and coughed on the heavy salt tinge. Calder's amused laughter crept into his thoughts like a cold rain.

Okay, Calder was meeting him, so this would probably be his best chance to get him out of town. He needed a plan of sorts, and he was hoping to capitalize on his friend's obvious misery or distress, whichever was most prevalent. Planning his strategy, he noticed a luxury car pull up next to him five minutes later, his partner beaming from behind the wheel.

"I can't believe it's you," Calder exclaimed as he pounded the steering wheel. "What are you doing here?"

Brody had to admit his partner looked fit and happy, something that took him by surprise. His Plan A disintegrated before his partner's big smile, and he scrambled to find Plan B.

"Who else would you expect to come driving into town?" That was a generous description of Sweetwater Harbor, but it worked for now. "Your two phone calls in the last month left a lot to the imagination." He could not hide the trace of irritation from his tone and was pleased when Calder had the decency to look ashamed. "After your last one, I had to come see what was going on for myself." He paused, feeling at a loss. "So, what exactly is going on?"

Calder chuckled. "Let's go to What If?, and I'll buy, then I can explain everything."

Dread curled around him as Calder pulled away. Brody gripped the wheel, helpless but to follow. Still mystified, Brody trailed Calder to a building on the edge of town sporting the colloquial signage of *What If?* Growing more puzzled, he shadowed Calder inside to a booth. He briefly glanced at the handful of midday patrons—three shooting pool, two throwing darts, and three others drinking at a table. He glanced at the menu, not hungry, and copied Calder's request to the server. Too many questions filled his mind. "So talk to me," Brody requested once drinks were poured, and orders were placed.

Calder smiled, big and happy. "I'm getting married."

"Yes, I know that. Penelope might expect you to be back home for the event, though." Too bad they couldn't just do the deed by conference call. He'd grab

Calder now and head to Vegas or somewhere civilized until after the wedding. In the end, Calder would thank him.

"Nope, not to her. Drink up. I have a lot to tell you."

Calder talked, explaining everything as Brody listened in shocked silence. "In your first phone call, you said you had some legal troubles," he finally pointed out, clearly missing a few of the pieces still. He dragged a fry through a puddle of ketchup and chewed slowly.

"Yes, I had been arrested. Because of Penelope."

"For what? Serving the wrong wine with dinner? Sneezing in public? Public shame on her?" While he didn't personally care for the socialite, he knew Calder did somewhat, though everyone assumed or knew the marriage was purely a business deal.

"No, it was a little more serious than that. She had a clever plan to frame me for Dad's murder, and even had me arrested. She had planned to have me sent to prison for life. It was to get all the wealth. She almost got away with it, too."

Brody considered that, surprised but not really. He'd always thought the woman was greedy and entirely too self-centered. He chewed another salty fry and swallowed it with cold soda. "But in your second call, you just said you planned to stay indefinitely here. That is quite a leap of differences between the two comments."

"River and her family are very rooted in this town. My town now. Well, our town. I promised River we would never ruin its quaint charm with heavy commercialism."

Brody blinked, choking on his drink. "Have you had a head injury lately? Do you need to see a doctor?" Thoughts swirled through Brody's mind. One, this might be the reason he needed to get his partner out of town, and secondly, he tried to wrap his mind around the consolation that Penelope would not be a regular fixture in his life anymore. That was a relief in and of itself.

"No, buddy, I'm just madly in love with River Gallagher and—"

Brody spat out his drink, spraying the plate of fries. "Gallagher. You're kidding, right?" He gagged, choking. "Gallagher? Does she have a sister by chance?" he asked once he could breathe again. He pushed the plate aside.

"Two of them. Why?"

Blotting his spilled drink, Brody explained about the spicy redhead from the plane.

Calder laughed; his hands splayed out. "Yes, that sounds about like Storm from what I hear. Sorry it had to be you she homed in on. You would not believe the first couple of meetings River and I had. She about killed me the first time."

If they were anything like his first meetings with Storm, yes, he would believe it. Even now, he could not get her flowing red hair, that beaded braid, her freckles, and laughing blue-green eyes out of his mind. Her sassy mouth, wet kisses, and hot lips pressed to his still seared his memory. Her trilling laugh and snappy comeback…oh, she was still filling his head hours later.

"Brody? Hey, man, you in there?"

Brody blinked, seeing Calder snapping his fingers before his face. Heat swept over his cheeks, and he cleared his throat. "Fine, I'm fine."

Calder gave him a dubious look. "So what happened when you met Storm?"

"She…I…that is…" Words utterly failed him as images at the drinking fountain swept over him like a small windstorm. "It was explosive," he finally offered. After that, it became unbelievable. Like a stick of dynamite blew up in his heart.

Calder nodded, slapping Brody on the shoulder. "I am so sorry, buddy. Of all the women in the world for you to meet, it had to be a Gallagher female. I am so sorry." Chuckling heartily, he pushed another soda over to his partner. "Take this, you're going to need it. Let's order a couple beers, too."

****

Storm shared a fruit tart with Raine, exclaiming it as sweet and fruity and perfect. She envied her sister the ability to create such delicate desserts and delicious meals from raw ingredients and her hands. If Storm tried this tart, she'd probably have fruity- colored play putty.

Raine shared her initial designs for the wedding cake.

Storm offered her opinions.

A few customers came in, welcoming Storm back.

Their tea and luncheon finished, Storm opted to head home, with Raine promising to bring dinner for everyone after she closed the shop. One final hug and Storm was back in her SUV, cruising through town.

She drove slowly, windows down, to take in the salty breeze and the waves of nostalgia, as she drove up Magnolia Lane to Finn Summit. Gulls and oystercatchers flew in the breeze. Amazing how memories all came back to her. But even now, her practiced eye took in the clouds and wind patterns, and she caught herself glancing back over her shoulder more than a few times. Maybe those goons had bothered her more than she liked to think. Was her research and data that valuable that they could show up here? Surely not. Either way, she planned how to keep her research hidden and her family safe.

Her parents' house greeted her like an old friend as she pulled in the drive, her home when she was between storms and disasters. Grabbing her duffle bags, she bounded up the steps, rapped at the door once, and twisted the handle. "Mom, Dad, I'm home!" Dropping her bags inside the door, she headed for the interior of the house, following the calls of "In here, dear."

They swept her into a shared hug.

Storm knew it was good to be home.

In short order, Muriel had laundry going.

Storm stepped into a shower, skin tingling at the sensation of hot water sluicing over her again. One downfall to active chasing was the complete lack of hot showers, regular home-cooked food, and a soft bed. Tonight, she would enjoy all of those, plus gathering with her family.

Drying off, Storm dressed in a sports bra and her last pair of clean shorts. They weren't much, she decided as she looked in the mirror, but they were clean and would get her by until her stuff was dried. "So Raine said she'd bring dinner by tonight," Storm said, returning to the spacious living room. "Can I assume River will come and bring her new intended?" Her lips twitched at the mere thought. Engaged. It still amazed her.

"Call and ask her," Muriel suggested as she dusted the rows of photos and assorted knickknacks. "I'm sure she will want to see you soon."

"Of course, we'll come," River said enthusiastically at Storm's question. "Calder's not around now, but he's already said he loves Raine's cooking better than mine."

Storm laughed. Everyone loved Raine's cooking. "She'll land a husband one day just for her baking and cooking skills. Even if she had the personality of a flat pancake." Except Raine also had the same Gallagher personality all the children had inherited from their parents. Raine could just be a little more subtle with hers. "Great. It will be good to see you and Calder again."

She hung up and hugged herself. She barely remembered the older boy from next door. "Did Frank and Lola's son hang out here a lot when we were kids?"

Cordell set his paper aside. "Some, but not all that much. I think he wanted to stay away from you girls and whatever cooties you might have."

His smile drew her over. She picked up a pillow from the sofa and tossed it at him, giggling as he caught it and tossed it back.

Muriel chuckled at their antics.

How good it felt to be home again.

****

Raine arrived first, bringing a little something she had quickly whipped together—*limone pollo tetrazzini* with frozen mocha tiramisu pie for their dessert. Storing it away, she settled in to visit with Storm and her parents until River and Calder arrived.

****

"Come on, we're going to be late," River insisted, stomping her foot.

Brody bit down on his lower lip. Between the human tornado Storm, and the brilliant bling of River, he was positive he was suffering from shock of some sort. If this persisted, he might require emergency care.

After Calder and Brody downed their beers at the bar with the funny name, Calder insisted on having him meet River. Okay, he had met Penelope, had not liked her much, and he figured by agreeing to meet this woman, he could use what he learned as additional ammo to get Calder the blazes out of town. Quickly. Before they had to share a meal with these people.

Except it wasn't working out that way. Right from the start, River Gallagher took his breath away as he entered the house and she swept him into a warm embrace, almost hugging the stuffing out of him.

"Calder never stops talking about you," she declared with a smile as bright as the glittering on her clothes. The sparkles in her silver T-shirt nearly blinded him. "He thinks the world of you, and we are both so happy you made it for the wedding."

"Yeah, about that—" he began awkwardly, until she grabbed his arm, pulling him away from Calder's side and toward the windows that overlook the ocean, or lake, or whatever body it was. He was getting lost not only in his head but in his bearings, as well.

"And now that you're here, of course you're going to stay and be his best man, aren't you? That will be wonderful. And we're going to Mom and Dad's tonight for some delicious dinner Raine is cooking." She hugged his arm, giving it a good pump. "You have to come," she insisted.

With his head spinning, and acutely aware of his partner's quiet smirk, he heard himself agreeing. To what he could only imagine. And now he found himself waiting alongside her, as his partner fiddled with something as he prepared for their dinner date.

"He's always fiddling with something," River lamented, casting sad eyes at him.

"That's Calder," Brody agreed mildly.

"You should see his neckties. Silliest collection I've ever seen."

"His collection back home is incredibly silly." Seems the guy wore a different one each day to the office and never the same one twice. Not that he had paid that much attention before but sitting next to River had a way of making him look at things differently. It must be something with the sparkle she emitted, both in dress and personality. He was beginning to see how his partner was swept away by her. Like a raging river, clear and swift. How deep did she go?

Calder gave them both a long-suffering sigh, adjusting his neckline. "At least one of us will show up at dinner looking presentable."

Brody barked a cough. "I had not planned on accepting any invitations while here," he muttered, casting a warning look at Calder.

"Come on you two." River jumped up and grabbed Brody's arm. "Enough. I can't wait for you to meet my family, Brody. You will have to tell us all about yourself."

He hesitated. "If Calder has talked about me, then you already know all there is."

River shook her head. "No, we want to hear about you, from you. That is different than his hero worship."

23

Hero worship? Taken aback by the comment, Brody allowed himself to be led out to the cars, aware of Calder's sudden silence. Had he missed something? Or was River just tossing a phrase in where it did not belong? Dismissing the thought for now, he reminded himself he needed to be properly prepared to weather meeting Storm again. And yet another sister, as well. And the parents. Oh dear God, what had Calder gotten them into?

They did not travel far, exchanging one house on stilts for another. One salty, ocean-swept beach for another. Two cars lined the driveway, a bright-blue, off-road boxy SUV with supersized tires that reached his knees and a license plate reading *KEEP CALM* and a little red-and-green British compact convertible wearing a regular North Carolina license plate. Contrasts. But not mules. Brody eyed them both warily. So which car belonged to which sister? Storm did not strike him as a particularly calm individual.

Wishing for another beer, hoping at least a strong drink would be offered, Brody braced himself for what probably would be the meeting to end all meetings. Catching his partner's amused grin, he shot him a silent frown before following him up the flight of steps.

Upon their arrival at the top, River knocked once before throwing the door open.

"We don't lock doors much around here," Brody heard Calder whisper near his ear. Clearly, he decided, amazed as he blindly followed them into the house. Not sure what to think, all thoughts flew from his mind as they rounded the hallway corner and entered a large, open room.

Telling himself the insane redhead sister would be

here was one thing. Seeing her, draped over the sofa, laughing with her father, and wearing next to absolutely nothing was quite another. Heat and thoughts rushed over him at the sight of her skin-tight, paper-thin shirt provocatively stretched over her pale skin. Skin that he knew from experience was rose-petal soft. Freckles dotted her exposed, plunging neckline. He inhaled sharply, and her fresh, sweet clean scent reached across the space to envelop him.

He felt the breath leaving his lungs in a sudden whoosh of shock, and then heat poured over him like molten lava as his body tightened in response. Did she have any clue how she looked right then?

Probably, with her. "Oh my God, woman," he stammered, nailed to the floor.

She lit up, rising to throw her arms around River in welcome before turning to run her gaze over Calder first and then settling on Brody. She ran her tongue over her lips.

Her movements and expressions added even more fuel to Brody's cranked-up heat. "Oh my God, woman," he repeated, his voice quaking.

Leaning back on the balls of her feet, she gave a laugh, her eyes dancing, hands going to the pockets of her incredibly short shorts. "Hello, lover."

Chapter Three

Brody sensed the stunned silence zapping through the room like lightning bolts following Storm's bold welcome. It felt like anything but a warm greeting. Memories of her full, wet kiss, and his body's reaction to hers at the drinking fountain swamped him, and heat spread through him.

"Lover?" Storm's father gave a hoot of laughter and slapped his knee. "I take it you two have met before?"

"Briefly." Storm evenly met Brody's gaze. "On the flight in."

Raine's lips twitched. "Love at thirty thousand feet?"

"Something like that," Storm agreed. "I needed his services."

Brody felt the heat burning the tips of his ears as the others laughed, imagining well what they thought from her description. Storm's amused expression and flickering eyes grated him. His body's reaction to her delight irritated him more. "It wasn't like that." He wished now he had grabbed Calder back at the marina and tossed him bodily into the car. They could be back home by now.

Calder laughed and slapped him on the back. "No, I'm sure it wasn't nearly as good as we're all thinking it was. But, buddy, just shut up, and let us have our imaginative way with it, okay?"

More heat fanned his neck and face as he stared at Storm, meeting her blue-green smiling stare.

"Everyone, this is Brody McGee, my partner and best buddy," Calder announced, his face lighting with unspoken emotions. "And soon to be my best man."

As introductions were complete, Brody wasn't sure he'd survive dinner, much less survive to a wedding. Muriel, matriarch and clearly accustomed to keeping control over a group of people, shuffled everyone into the spacious dining room and to their assigned seating. As he sank into the chair she indicated as his, he had to wonder if fate or something else equally cruel placed him next to Storm.

Cordell cleared his throat. "Storm, surely you can find something to put on before you join us?"

Brody could have happily shaken the man's hand.

She returned a moment later with a gauzy, green linen blouse knotted at her waist that highlighted the green in her eyes. She slid into her seat and gave Brody a short giggle.

"Did the airline lose your luggage?" he asked, leaning close and getting a strong whiff of floral extracts and damp hair laden with the scent of fresh berries and coconut. He surprised himself by liking the mixture.

"Nope, just getting caught up on my laundry. Working in the field, I don't see many commercial laundries."

Another point to prove how insane her career choice was. If one could not readily find self-service laundries and washing facilities at the end of the day, surely something was amiss.

Raine set a steaming casserole dish in the center of the table while Muriel laid out twin baskets of bread and colorful vegetables.

Heat escaped, rising into the air, filling the room with the aroma of spices, yeast, and butter.

"Eat up, everyone." Muriel patted his shoulder before sitting down. "Raine has made plenty."

Brody shot Calder a glance, aware he was seated next to his intended.

Calder raised his glass to Brody, grinned happily, and picked up his napkin.

"Now, Brody, dear, don't be shy," Muriel encouraged. "Dig in."

If anyone else caught the endearment, they gave no indication. But he clearly heard it and wondered at it. Perhaps it was just her way? Like a sweet old grandma who liked to fuss over her brood. Something he had heard of but never actually experienced before.

"And tell us all about yourself," River urged around bites. "Raine, this is great!"

"There isn't much to tell," Brody hedged, aware of Storm's sharp gaze on him. He tried to shrug it off by scooping up the creamy casserole. It smelled good, rich with lemons and herbs. "Surely, Calder has already told you all he can." By now, in the weeks his partner had spent with these people, he could only assume Calder probably blabbed his deepest secrets. Seeing he was being integrated into the family unit was obvious. That would make it harder to get him away and back home, but not impossible. He simply had to reconfigure his plan.

"Doubtful," Storm scoffed. "You have an Irish or Scottish name, too. Like us. Which one are you?"

He shook his head. "I have no idea." His parents never spoke of their ancestry or where their name came from. They divorced when he was young, and he spent his growing-up years shuttled across the country between them. His mom clearly disdained the McGee side of the family, and his dad apparently never cared enough to mention it. As a result, he had no interest in his genealogy and no belief in the fragile and misleading institution of marriage. Not that he had any intention of sharing any of that information with these people.

"It would not be hard to start finding out. There are all sorts of online groups that do that," Raine offered.

Brody favored the youngest sister with a smile and a shake of his head. She was cute, wore her dark hair in a chic bob, carried herself with a lively energy, and was easily the most congenial of the three. "Thanks, but honestly, it doesn't matter to me where I came from or who was in my past. I am more concerned with where I am going and what is in my future." Even as he spoke the words, he noticed the amused grin of one spicy redhead. He fought off the urge to squirm at her clear interest in his personal life.

River cleared her throat. "So where are your parents, Brody? Where did you grow up?"

He swallowed back the sigh building in his throat. They were so nosy! People in Atlanta never interrogated him like this. "One lived in Boston, and the other in California. I spent my years traveling between them." He heard the *tsk* of sympathy from Muriel and turned his attention to his plate. It really was good food, and he had not realized how hungry he was. If they caught the past tense in how he referred to his parents, they chose not to pursue it. At least not yet.

"Let the man enjoy his meal in peace," Cordell said, shaking a finger around the table.

Brody could have hugged him.

"You can give him the Spanish Inquisition later on, after his dinner's digested some."

Great, simply great. He shot Calder a strained look.

Calder only grinned and took another mouthful of buttered bread.

Wonderful. He owed his partner a punch in the jaw at the very least. Thanks to Cordell's order, he was spared further grilling. The conversation simply shifted to new topics.

They talked of small-town gossip, plans for the wedding, the weather, and boats.

Brody listened, savoring the meal and making notes on the people surrounding him. Though nosy, they were also interesting. The bond between Muriel and Cordell was as tangible to see as though it were tied in silken cord. Again, he felt that sense of awe of here was someone, flesh-and-blood proof, of long-lasting, love-filled marriages. The fairy-tale stuff he knew seldom existed.

Raine was a fantastic cook and certainly was less impetuous than her sisters, who tended to shoot off random comments. Her dark hair, cut in a chic bob layered to her chin, accented her petite features. River, for all her sparkling bling, stared at his partner as if the sun and moon rose and set on him. Every word he added to the conversation was hung onto like golden jewels. How did Calder get so lucky and score a woman who was into him like that? He never recalled the former fiancée offering Calder much of a chance to speak at her social events, much less listen when he did express an opinion. Here, Brody saw a value to what his partner thought, beyond the boardroom and meeting room walls.

That knowledge shook him. No doubt Calder was appreciating this and would not be too eager to leave it behind.

And lastly, there was the red-haired Storm. Her blue-green eyes slid over him as frequently as her red tongue licked up creamy sauce from her full lips. He remembered those flaming lips, coated in fruity lip gloss, and pressed so firmly to his. If he wasn't careful, he'd choke on his dinner. When he caught her sending him a flirty wink over her wineglass, he all but gagged on the piece of chicken thigh he'd been swallowing. The brassy minx was a hot mess of pure trouble. And desirable enough to ignite his imagination, now that she had already touched a lot of his buttons.

The quicker he got away from her, the better. "Raine, this is very good," he praised, trying to ignore Storm. "Have you studied culinary arts abroad by any chance?"

"No." She shook her head, smiling at the compliment. "Mom taught me how to read a recipe in a cookbook when I was younger. That is all it took."

He sampled another bite. "I have friends back home who would love to know someone who can cook this well, without having been formally trained by master chefs. You have a gift." His words made her blush, adding to her cuteness, and her parents smiled and grinned at one another, evidently pleased with his praise of their youngest.

****

Once dinner and a sweet dessert of tiramisu pie was complete, Storm, River, and Raine cleared the table, joining their mother in the kitchen. Soon the sounds of clanking dishes, laughter, and bantering filled the room.

"Storm, you didn't need dessert," Raine giggled. "You were about to eat up Brody McGee."

Storm snapped a towel at her sister's hip, smiling at the accusation and how Raine darted out of the way. "So?"

"So?" River stood at the counter, pouring leftovers into bowls. She leveled a stare at her sister and wagged her index finger. "You called him lover. What gives with you two?"

"Absolutely nothing. Like I said, I just needed to hire his services for a short while." She took the first dish River handed her, scrubbed it once, and handed it to Raine. "But it's fun to speculate." She paused, thinking of the term she wanted. "He's interesting," she finally decided.

"He's hot." Raine frowned as she scratched a fingernail over another dish Storm just handed her. She handed it back. "That's still dirty."

"From what Calder said, he sort of has a bitter view of love and marriage and all that," River said slowly.as she replaced the condiments and napkins to their places.

Storm rolled her eyes at Raine and then smiled broadly at River. "All the better." She plunged the pan back into the sudsy water and scrubbed it again.

"Now, Storm, don't do anything that would harm him," Muriel warned as she burped the plastic containers stacked along the counter.

"Mom, I would never dream of it. He seems like a

big enough boy that he can handle a little bit of fun."
He had so far.

Muriel paused. "Just be sure you can handle it if you push him too far and he decides to come back with his own set of rules to the game."

At that, Storm laughed. "That will be the day I can't handle what a man brings to me." From the moment she pressed her body to his, holding him fast for that sweet kiss, she wanted to know what else he was capable of. What would it take to find out?

"Storm…"

"Yeah, Mom. He seems like a kind man. I won't hurt him." She just didn't know what kind of man Brody was. But she was looking forward to finding out more. And she was very glad he was on hand to assist when she needed to borrow him to escape the goons at the airport. What if they had followed her to Sweetwater Harbor and home?

****

Brody joined Calder and Cordell on the back porch once the women assembled in the kitchen. Calder assured him they would be cleaning up for a little while.

Cordell pulled up his Adirondack chair and withdrew his pipe, lighting it.

Calder sat, cradling his wineglass.

Brody preferred to stay standing, politely refusing the offered chair. Instead, he leaned against the railing, taking in the rolling ocean surf tinged with the strong scents of mint and briny salt and other things he could scarcely identify. Birds flew overhead, calling loudly.

In his fingers, he, too, gripped a wineglass. Conscious of his hold on it, he set it down, lest he accidentally break the thin stem. Listening to Calder and Cordell talk, his mind sorted through the last few hours.

Seeing Calder was firmly meshed in here, with his new intended and the Gallagher family, was crystal clear. Brody had every confidence that Calder glowed in the acceptance he enjoyed with them and would fight not to leave. Brody swallowed back a heavy sigh. This was not going as he had planned. From the moment he met that fiery stormy redhead, his life had quickly left the planned path, and he almost felt too lost to find it now. How had such a simple strategy gone so far astray?

"Brody, you going to join us tonight or not?"

Calder's words broke into his tumbled thoughts of stormy women. Turning, he saw his partner nodding at the other chair, and he wrinkled his brows together. Brody knew that look. Forcing back a moan, he complied.

"I was just saying," Cordell said. "Winter will be home soon."

"Winter?" Had he missed another family member? Heaven help him if it was yet another crazy redhead.

"My son. And Storm's twin brother. He's currently serving in the Army overseas but has leave time saved to come for River and Calder's wedding."

Brody could not mistake the joy in Cordell's face and voice. With all the females strutting around, he probably lived for when his son could return. Perhaps that was why he so readily adopted Calder, as a substitute for his son and a male relief from the outnumbering females. What did Calder get from it? He knew Calder had not been remarkably close to his own dad. "That's good," Brody murmured, still deep in thought. "Did he mention how long he would be staying?" As far as he could see, the longer the son stayed, the better for him. Maybe if Winter were integrated back into the family, Calder would slowly assimilate back out. Maybe all he had to do was bide his time.

Cordell shook his head. "No, he didn't mention any time frame. Just said we could expect him soon." He took a long puff on his pipe. "You two boys should get along well with Winter."

Brody perked up, glancing over at Calder. Get along? Was he as crazy as his sisters?

"He's a mite younger than you two, especially you, Calder, but he can help deflect some of the energy coming from his sisters."

Brody was starting to like him already. He caught the subtle smile on the old man's face and again glanced over at Calder. Poor guy had three sisters to contend with, so he must be a bastion of strength. No wonder he was overseas. Brody was spared any further comment as Muriel and her daughters filed out onto the porch.

"What a lovely evening," Muriel commented. "Perhaps we should all walk along the beach?"

Her suggestion was met with majority favor, and Brody found himself joining the group as they all trooped down the winding wooden steps to the sandy shore. The wind picked up and assaulted him afresh with both ocean scent and wave sound. Chatter and laughter ruled, so once again Brody could observe in relative silence, offering comments only when specifically required to.

The family questioned Storm regarding her current work, and she answered, but even Brody could sense a touch of hesitancy in some of her answers. He tried to tell himself what she was doing out chasing various storms was none of his business; yet, he still found himself drawn to her, for a few reasons.

He liked the fact she held mysteries, even from her own family, whom she clearly loved dearly. Without being defensive, she cleverly avoided certain questions, deflecting them artfully away to safer subjects. He admired that trait. He also felt drawn to her strong beauty. While all three sisters were easy on the eyes, Storm was different in her strength and undisputable courage. She needed a lot of guts to single him out at the airport and do what she had done. She might laugh it off as no big deal, but few women—or men, for that matter—would have had the courage to even try such a crazy stunt. It had not been without risk.

So what was the desperate motivation for her to even attempt it? What had prompted her to need his services, as she so quaintly put it to the others? What had he unknowingly helped her with? Was the lovely redhead in some sort of danger? Was that what caused the caginess in some of her answers to their nosy questions?

Interesting. Suddenly, Brody was seeing this brassy minx in a whole new light.

"That's a curious smile you have there, Brody McGee." Storm walked over on the sand. She stuck her hands on the back pockets of her shorts and eyed him speculatively.

"Really? I hadn't noticed." Quickly, he smothered it by studying the moon rising over the water's edge.

Boats returned to the harbor, lights blinking as they chugged past. Cordell, Muriel, and River waved at a few of the drivers.

"Yeah, really." Storm lifted her hair off her neck.

Brody tried not to notice how the thin green fabric stretched over the flimsy material of her sports bra. Again, he shifted his focus back to the boats and water and moon, drawing in a deep breath. The smell of salt air blew away the floral and berry scents of her bath soap.

"So what do you think of our little town?" she asked.

Calder's town, wasn't it? From what he understood, Calder had inherited most of the sandy seclusion. "It's different than I am used to," he answered simply, still trying to keep his gaze off her. When had he and Storm become separated from the rest of the group? She and he stood barely two feet apart, while the others had moved on farther up the beach. Seeking a safe distance, he took a step in the only direction he could, closer to the water's edge.

"Maybe we should return to the Spanish Inquisition," she suggested, smiling, her eyes lighting up. "If your meal is properly digested by now, of course."

She was baiting him again. In a different time in his life, he might have enjoyed matching wits with this wild woman. Back in Atlanta where he had both the home court advantage and the luxury of time on his hands. Right now, he had neither.

She licked her lips. "So tell me, what took you to Georgia? It's a far cry from Boston and California."

"Actually, it's geographically close to the middle

37

of them," he said, taking another step back. In a scenic route direction, he was completely right. Though that wasn't the excuse as why he settled there, making it his home state now. He didn't care to get into lengthy explanations now. She wasn't the only one who could deflect unwanted conversation.

"Oh, I know my geography. Probably better than you do even," she assured.

Her smile hinted that she knew he was hedging.

"I'm just curious what made you pick Georgia to settle in."

Why did it matter if he shared the basic truth with her? "The real estate opportunities offered a lot." He hoped that explanation ended her curiosity. He was growing uncomfortable with the entire conversation. Where was that brother at? When was he arriving? Soon couldn't be quick enough. He cast a glance up the beach, as if that would magically bring the man suddenly walking along the sand. "So I hear your brother will be arriving soon. You two are twins?"

She nodded. "We are. Fraternal. I'm the older by two minutes."

He didn't doubt that. Any man in his right mind would be wise to let her go first, even babies in the womb. His respect for this mystery brother was growing in leaps and bounds. "Your father will be glad to see him arrive. He strikes me as needing another male presence around here."

Storm drew back, her eyes growing wide. "My father does not need anything." A hint of defensive venom laced her comment with warning.

Backpedaling, aware he might have crossed a line, Brody looked around for support. The rest of the group was still clustered about forty feet away, chatting and laughing as they watched the setting sun. Brody held his hands out to Storm. Riled, though he didn't know why, he had to admit she was a formidable-looking woman. The sea breeze picked up her hair and swirled it around her. "All I meant was it might do your father good to have some male company around him occasionally. Guys like having other guys around them."

She took that in, her mouth quirking. "So why don't you hang out and be my dad's guy pal?"

"Because I have things to do. I think your father is a neat guy, but I have my own plans." Plans he was rapidly losing track of. Plans he needed to quickly reformulate and implement.

"Such as?"

Oh no, he wasn't going for that one. He smiled at her question and then shook his head. "Things I can't talk about now."

"I thought you came to town for the wedding?"

"I did," he answered, hedging it neatly. Not a lie, he had come for the wedding, just not in the way she would be expecting.

"You don't have any crazy ideals, do you?" She folded her arms.

He started. "No, of course not. Like what?" He blinked, surprised, and a healthy dose of concern snaked down his back in a warning as her eyes went from blue to storm-green.

"You tell me."

He grew rock solid and felt a sudden chill. His mouth went dry. He tried for a laugh, not quite making it. "I've nothing to tell you. Besides, I am not the only one being a little evasive here."

She met his subtle challenge with a jutted chin. "Do you plan to hurt my family?"

The question came out in a low whisper. A suggested threat. Her stormy eyes narrowed to mere slits. "No, of course not." A hot slice of sharp unease rolled over him, stalling his breath. She pinned him to the sandy beach as strong emotions rolled over him.

"If you do—" she began. Suddenly she unfurled her arms, placing the palms of her hands against his chest and gave a powerful shove.

Stunned, Brody staggered, his arms flapping helplessly as he propelled back through the wet sand, landing in the cold ocean. Waves washed over him. Shocked, he inhaled, sputtering, and gagging as the salt water filled his eyes, nose, and throat.

Chapter Four

Storm stomped up the steps and into the house. She heard Raine follow her and considered shutting the door on her face.

"Lover's spat?" Raine caught the door in her grip.

Storm huffed, ignoring the question. Or was it a barb? She rolled her eyes. The rest of the family had immediately cloistered around Brody, pulling him from the ocean. But for whatever unknown reason, Raine deemed it better to follow her…and dog her every step.

They raced through the house, Raine only a few steps behind, to the laundry room. Storm skidded to a halt and yanked laundry from the dryer, searching for something dry enough to wear. Discarding garments into a pile, she finally found a pair of capris. She slipped them on over her mini shorts and stuffed the rest back into the dryer. Then she returned to the living room and snatched up her bag.

"Going somewhere?"

"Yes, away from Brody McGee." Storm tried to push her way past Raine, but her younger sister made herself into a solid wall.

Raine nodded. "So you two did have a lover's spat."

"No! We're not lovers."

Raine snorted in clear disbelief.

"We only just kissed. That's all." Of which, she

was grateful for, but still… "Oh, never mind. Get out of my way, kid."

Raine slid out of her path. And reach. "Lovers usually kiss," she pointed out mildly.

Storm whirled back. "He asked for it."

Raine grinned. "The kiss or the dunking?"

"The dunking. Both. I don't know. But he asked for it. Now move it!"

"Sure he did." Raine smirked as she moved ever so slightly.

Moving past her sister, Storm went outside. She needed air! She went down the steps, two at a time, to her SUV. She climbed inside, hit the headlights, and backed out of the driveway, heading for anywhere Brody McGee was not. Replaying Raine's questions, she could not answer them. Nor could she help what she'd just done. Between Brody's ambiguous comment and defensive posture, she could only see those goons coming to town. Her mom might say she overreacted just now, and she winced, knowing it could be true on some occasions, but not now.

While she considered herself normally a grounded person, fear overtook her better judgment, and she pictured the unknown thugs harming her family for her important data. She could not sacrifice one to save the other. She would not.

Torn between anger at the thought such a possibility could exist and the strong desire to protect what was hers, she simply reacted instinctively. By shoving away the one thing that created such negative emotions—Brody McGee.

Now, in hindsight, she realized he most likely had nothing to do with her data, but she had failed to see that through the red mist clouding her eyes. She was only looking to protect and defend. Seeing his startled expression as he landed with a giant splash and hearing the gasping cry of her mother, sharply calling "Storm Diana!" she had whirled for the house. Now, after the fact, perhaps an apology might have been better, instead of taking off. But if she had, it would not have been sincere.

Right now, these thoughts nipping at her like River's two terrier dogs, she needed to get away. If those goons did come to town, what was she going to do?

****

Stunned, coughing, and spitting salty ocean water, Brody stared in disbelief at Storm's backside as she raged up the shore, sand flying beneath her feet as her fast strides carried her up the steps and into the house, quickly followed by her younger sister.

Calder gripped his arms and hauled him from the cold water.

The others closed in, murmuring apologies, and asking way too many questions.

"I don't know," he repeated as the briny water burned his throat. He coughed again, ending in a wheezy gag. Had she just tried to kill him? What had he said to make her push him like that? Crazy, impulsive woman! She could turn on a dime with her moods!

"You're shivering," Muriel observed, her hand resting gently on his shoulder. "You need to get out of those soaked clothes this minute."

Cordell nodded. "Storm's a testy little thing. Did you say something to set her off, lad?"

Testy? He thought that was testy. Oh boy.

43

Explosive seemed more appropriate. Set her off, like a lit powder keg.

Muriel had his arm, River taking his other arm, and the two of them dragging him to the steps. "I'm fine, really." He tried to shake off their concern. "I can change later."

"Pooh to you. Salt water is nothing to mess with." Muriel brushed off his protest like grains of sand.

"I...my clothes are in my car, back at Calder's." He faltered, feeling the shivering chill setting in now. To keep his teeth from chattering, he clamped his jaws.

"Do you even have a place to stay tonight, dear? Somewhere to go and change clothes?"

He looked away. He hadn't planned on needing a place to stay the night. He had planned on being on the way back home by now, with Calder in tow. So much for Plan A or Plan B for that matter. Thanks to that crazy Storm, he would be lucky to end up with a Plan J, K, L, or M that worked for him.

"Now, don't you worry, Brody dear. We have some things of Winter's that will work fine for now. You can bring them back later. We can't have you catch your death of cold."

Wasn't Muriel the very one who had pointed out earlier how pleasant an evening it was? Something inside him wilted, surrendering. Stepping inside the house, he felt a rush of gratefulness for the warmth.

"So now it's settled," Muriel said, releasing his arm. "Upstairs with you now, and no more arguments. I'll have Calder bring you some things."

"Where is Storm?" Brody looked around. His heart slammed against his chest at the thought of seeing her so soon.

"Where else? She's stormed off again," River remarked dryly. She released the curtain she'd lifted to look out over the driveway, and turned back, lifting her shoulder in a shrug.

Figures, he decided thickly. Going to the room Muriel had instructed, he waited, shivering, and bewildered. He considered dragging the blanket off the bed to wrap around his shoulders. Instead, he stared out the window. Both the blue SUV and the subcompact car were gone. Both relief and a slice of disappointment knifed through him. Storm Diana. He stared at the empty parking spaces as her mother's tone rolled through his mind. The names suited her. Diana, the mythological Roman goddess of the hunt, the moon, and birthing.

He had always had an interest in Roman and Greek mythology and knew Diana to be associated with wild animals, supposedly able to communicate with them. The maiden was one of three sworn never to marry and had control over the woodlands. She was not a goddess to be trifled with. He smirked. Cordell might consider the goddess Diana to be testy.

Yeah, he blew out a breath; Storm Diana fit his daughter well. A knock at the door drew his attention.

Calder came in, carrying a short stack of folded clothes and wearing a big smile.

"Thanks for the help back there, partner," Brody snapped, grabbing the extended pile of clothes.

Calder leaned back against the wall with his arms folded. "I like living," he drawled.

He stripped and hastily redressed. "So do I."

"Upsetting Storm doesn't seem to be a way to live healthy. Or long."

Brody shot him a dark glare, as he yanked up the zipper on the jeans. They fit well. And, most importantly, they were warm and dry.

"Empty your pockets," Calder instructed. He held out a small plastic bag. "Muriel wants your wet stuff back to wash. She said it's the least she can do for her daughter trying to drown you in the Atlantic."

Brady threw him another thunderous look, tossing his dripping clothes into the plastic bag once he removed his keys, wallet, cell phone and empty gum wrapper. Would his phone even work now? Hopefully, the case kept it dry.

Calder shrugged as he took the sack. "Muriel has a motherly nature. Get used to it."

"You know this was utter insanity, right? What are we doing here?"

"It seems to me once Winter arrives, you and I are going to have to take him out and treat him to a dinner."

"Why?" And why was Calder ignoring his question?

"I wore those same clothes for a few days."

Wondering the reason, he pulled a thick, warm sweater on. "Hopefully, they've been washed since then," he commented dryly. As the cabled sweater slid over his face, he inhaled the fresh floral fragrance of laundry detergent.

Calder ignored the barb like he'd ignored Brody's comment. "Did I happen to mention how River and I first met? She attacked me with a baseball bat."

"It figures." Apparently both sisters were equally bold, impulsive, and beautifully dangerous.

Calder tried unsuccessfully to smother his grin. "It was Storm's bat." He glanced around the room. "I'd bet this is her room, too. She stays here between chases, I guess."

Fully redressed and slowly warming, Brody spun in a circle, taking in the room. Baseball pendants and Carolina college posters decorated the walls. A queen-sized bed was covered with a deep-blue, swirled spread. A leather bomber jacket and ball caps hung on a wooden coatrack. It was neat and not what he would consider a woman's bedroom, except for the small dressing table tucked in the corner. The pink ruffled seat, assorted hair bands, and little bottles of stuff neatly lined up spelled woman all right. And provided a sharp contrast to the sports décor.

Cutting Calder another dark look, Brody walked over and picked up a couple of bottles. One was perfume, and one was nail polish. Setting the bright-red bottle back, he uncapped the seashell-shaped glass and sniffed. Pretty, without being overpowering. It seemed incredibly tame for her. Replacing it, he stepped to the closet and pulled the door open.

Sweats and chambray shirts shared equal space with faded jeans and assorted T-shirts. He glanced at the labels, noting they were not designer, but not super cheap, either. Somewhere in the middle. How conventional for her. Why hadn't she worn one of these to dinner, instead of that provocative blouse? Worn tennis shoes and sandals lay piled on the floor in no matching order, and a few more ball caps lined the shelf beside a couple of cardboard boxes. About to pull a box down, he reconsidered. Sliding the door closed, he turned back.

Calder watched him, arms folded and an amused grin on his face. "Done snooping?" he asked mildly.

"Man, what did that girl do to you?"

"She pushed me into the wretched ocean," he retorted, heat building in his face. "You were there." He snatched up his bag of wet clothing Calder had left on the bed and elbowed past Calder to head for the stairs.

"I meant before that," Calder explained, trailing behind him.

Brody bit back several retorts, refusing to be baited into a verbal parry-and-thrust discussion with Calder. That volatile redhead was messing with his mind too much to think logically for a word dance with his partner.

****

Her family was safe, and Brody would be fine, and her data was secure. Those were the important things to concentrate on for now. Storm pulled in a calming breath, stared at the ocean waves, and reminded herself of these basic facts. All was good. She was home for River's wedding, and then she could deliver her data and move on with her life. On to the next chase. Mother Nature wasn't needed to provide her with a storm somewhere.

Brody McGee would do whatever he was in town for and move on with his life and move out of hers.

Deep breath in, watch the waves rolling in, let the deep breath out, and repeat. She heard a familiar whistle and closed her eyes. Slow exhale. "Why'd you follow me, Raine?" she asked, without turning around.

Raine settled herself on the bumper of the SUV next to her. " 'Cause I wanted to," she answered simply, glancing once at Storm, their gazes catching for one more moment, before both turning back to the water.

" 'Cause you wanted me to."

Storm smiled. Yeah, deep in her heart, she had wanted Raine right now. Bratty little kid sister always knew her heart. "We did not have a lover's spat," she declared flatly. "We are not lovers."

"Okay, fine. You did not have a lover's spat, and you're not lovers. Got it." Raine never turned from the water.

But Storm noticed her pressing her tongue firmly into her cheek. The cheeky brat was most likely going to try needling her again.

After a moment, Raine spoke. "He's just a silly sod who happened to upset you…by…?"

"Breathing?" Storm suggested dryly. Already, she was wishing she could steal his breath away with another long kiss. Evidently, she had enjoyed the last ones a little too much.

Raine gasped, hand going to her chest. "How dare he! The unmitigated gall to breathe around you. The horror of it all!" She paused before adding, "Did he not even ask permission first?"

Storm reached out, shoving her off the bumper.

Raine laughed and climbed back up, unfazed.

"You haven't changed a bit," Storm accused.

"Nope. And neither have you. So, what's gotten you so edgy? You were holding back at dinner."

Storm sighed, pulling at her hair. Did she have another ponytail holder in the console?

"You're ignoring me."

She stepped off the bumper, going to the door, and riffling around inside, looking for an elastic band.

Raine followed suit, opening the passenger door and leaning across the seat. "You're not going to

49

answer me, are you?"

"Doesn't look like it, kiddo." Storm found a blue band and twirled it around her hair, then returned to the bumper.

Raine joined her, linking arms as they silently watched the moon sparkle off the waves.

While she would love to confess everything to Raine, it was safer for everyone if she did not.

****

Brody handed his bag of wet clothes over to Muriel, offering an awkward thank you.

She smiled, patted his arm, and walked away with his laundry.

"Here you go, lad. This will wash down that salty taste," Cordell said, passing over a glass.

The glass did not hold the same red wine they'd had at dinner. He sniffed and then took a swallow. The liquid was instantly cool and soothing, easing the stinging burn in his throat. Smiling, he took a seat with Cordell and Calder in the living room. Cordell had a fire blazing in the fireplace. Brody needed a minute to realize the fire was electric powered. He set the glass down and wiped his mouth. "That was good."

"Mostly milk." Cordell nodded, giving a wink. "And a few other things. But mostly milk. Now, what happened that my daughter tried to drown you?"

Brody shrugged. "I don't know. We were talking, and next thing I know, she's pushing me into the water."

Cordell sighed, then looked out the window and back to Brody. "Life's most perplexing problems tend to come along in the form of people."

Yes, that was true, he supposed. Unsure how to

answer, he was glad to see Muriel return, dusting her hands off.

"Those will be washed and dry tomorrow. Stop by sometime then, and you can pick them up, Brody," she said. "Now then, what had you considered about arrangements for your time in town?"

Brody faltered. He hadn't thought about it yet. But it was getting late, and he wasn't leaving town without Calder coming along. "I don't know. I guess I can get a room at that inn. I came into town and spotted a sign. I think it was called the Golden Anchor?"

"Nonsense," Calder protested. "You're staying with River and me. We have plenty of room."

Muriel beamed. "Well, that's all settled then."

"Don't worry, lad," Cordell chuckled. "Once you think you have the world on a string, someone is bound to show up with a pair of scissors."

Yes, that's how it was tending to go. And it had all started with that spicy redhead. Would she be around when he returned tomorrow for his clothing?

****

Storm arose, selecting a favorite pair of jeans she had left behind on the last trip and a blue-and-white jersey T-shirt from the closet. Mom would have breakfast about done. Already, she could smell coffee brewing and sausage frying. The intoxicating scents drifted upstairs, poking her to wakefulness. "Morning, Mom. Hi, Dad," she greeted, swinging down the stairs and dropping into a chair. "Isn't it a lovely day? Not an angry cloud in the sky."

Cordell smiled as he dug into his pancakes. "I would have thought you'd find a day like today dull and boring."

"Not at all." She poured liberal syrup over her pancakes. "It just means I am free to do something else beyond chase."

"Such as?"

"I'd like to take the bike out for a spin. It probably needs a tune up." Her motorcycle, a classic Harley, was her baby. Built for riding and plenty of it, she could never take it out enough.

Muriel set a plate of steaming sausage down and filled Storm's cup with coffee. "Brody will be by sometime to collect his laundry. You ought to apologize for your behavior last night."

She chewed thoughtfully, ignoring her mom's tsk tone and delaying having to respond. A slice of excitement raced over her. Would he show up while she was still home, tinkering with the bike? He didn't seem the kind who thought girls should have bikes and masculine things like that. Did he think girls just played with toy dollies all the time and had pretend tea parties?

She smiled. Oh, she could give him a lesson on what girls liked to play with next time she saw him. Some girls liked motorcycles and knew how to make them run.

"Storm?"

"Yeah, Mom. I'll talk to him," she promised and took another bite.

Muriel let out a sigh, sitting down and filling her own plate. "Storm, Brody is a nice man. Make sure your apology isn't sandwiched between something else."

Storm raised her brows. "Like what?"

"Like something only you could dream up."

Storm hid her grin. How well her mom knew her!

Like the time she stole Winter's clothes and made him walk home in just his underwear from a friend's house—in another town, of course. She had no end to the things she could do. And—naturally—her apologies sometimes fell short of true contrition. She apologized to Winter for the prank—sort of. She could ask forgiveness from Brody, too, but if he expected to hear silky words of "I'm sorry," he would probably be disappointed.

****

Brody stared at the little white dog that lay staring up at Calder as if he were an idol. Both dogs lay obediently in their beds while the three humans dined. The white one was clearly Calder's shadow. Last night, just before they had all retired, he and Calder took a few moments to catch up, and Brody was struck with the peaceful scene of the dog lying snuggled in Calder's lap and snoring softly. "I didn't think you liked dogs much, Calder. Not after what had happened with Sophie's monster." He had commented last night.

Calder shrugged and snapped his fingers. "Ah, right, her name had been Sophie. I'd already forgotten her name and almost her face." He grinned at Brody. "I tell you, buddy. River fills up all my mental images these days." He shrugged again at the dog. "I don't care for dogs, but Salt adopted me."

"Salt?"

"Yeah. The black one is Pepper."

Despite how little he liked the direction their conversation was going, he still had to smile at the dog's names. "So it adopted you? Isn't that supposed to work the other way around?"

Calder just sighed, stroking the snoozing dog.

"Well, normally it might, I guess. But Sweetwater Harbor isn't a place where things always go normal or as planned."

"Yeah, I'm beginning to see that." The place had scissors ready to cut his well-planned strings at regular intervals. And what would the next day bring was all he could think of as he finally drifted off to sleep in River's guest room. His partner had inherited a quirky, interesting town, and he had inherited a huge headache from getting him back home to Atlanta. He took a drink of wine before continuing the conversation, trying to find an out.

"Your dad's house is just over a few...streets." Another strong word. But what was he supposed to call the sandy trails between houses? He waved in the general direction he meant. "Why do you stay here?"

A pained look crossed Calder's face.

Brody wondered if he was going to answer.

"It's unsettling to be in the house." Calder shook his head. "I still can't be in there and not...you know."

No, Brody didn't know, and the look in Calder's eyes convinced him he didn't want to. He brushed a chill aside and tried again. "When did you say you and River had to go out of town for the trial of Penelope?" He tried but could not imagine the diva in jail. She was probably giving the jailors fits for all the things not up to her high standards. Knowing her, that list would be long.

Calder groaned and stroked the wiry dog. "Next week. This isn't the actual trial yet, but it's some court hearing for bail and to set future dates. River absolutely swore she'd raise heaven and earth if Penelope got out on bail." Calder grinned humorlessly. "Nothing like attending the trial of your ex-fiancée to testify against her, along with your new fiancée, less than ten days before your wedding."

"Timing could be better." Brody had to agree the irony and timing were not the best. They also added to his concern of how to get Calder home. Last night, he'd checked the county courthouse and jail locations on his map app and saw they were twenty miles south of Sweetwater Harbor. He fell asleep, hoping some great plan would come to him during the night about how to use Calder being out of town soon to keep him from returning.

Now, in the light of day, no clear answers to his nighttime questions, Brody pushed his empty plate away. "River, that was delicious. I suppose I should go over to your parents' place and pick up my clothes."

River reached for the dishes and grinned. "Storm would be up and about by now. Surely, she would be starting some project or another."

Curious, he still refused the bait. He had no interest in whatever projects that crazy woman might be into. Something dangerous and insane, no doubt. Fireworks? Explosives? He would not be surprised. "Well, either way, your mother instructed me to stop by. Now is as good a time as ever."

"You and I can catch up later, once River goes on to Watercolors, where our property management offices are," Calder promised, shooting his soon-to-be wife a wide smile. "Maybe grab lunch at What If? again."

River slid into Calder's outstretched arm, and they shared a kiss, giggling when it ended.

Brody could not recall a single time Penelope Socialite ever showed a public display of affection with

Calder. "Sure, sounds good." Brody looked at the passionate expressions Calder and River shared. They were knit together so tight; he didn't know how he'd ever get Calder out of town. He fished his cell phone out of the bag of rice River had wrapped it in last night, tested the signal strength, and wondered how leaving here would affect Calder. How deep River's roots ran in this town was impossible to miss. Or how attached Calder and River were. Leaving the giggling, cuddling couple, he snagged his jacket and headed down the stairs to the briny breeze.

Brody took the scenic route to the Gallagher house, following the shoreline for a full five minutes. The view was completely different than what he was used to. He looked around at the sea and sand and boats and tried to wrap his head around that Calder had grown up here. He passed the Finn house, now empty. Calder mentioned he still felt unnerved going there, which was why he preferred staying at River's in her spare room. Lucky, she had two of them. He had some work to do when he felt up to it but wasn't in any hurry as they'd stay at her place once they were married, and he had no immediate plans for the Finn house.

Great, that did not bode well for making plans to return to Atlanta soon. They needed to discuss this matter today. Giving the wheeling seagulls and crashing waves one more look, Brody stopped behind a supersized blue SUV with a bumper sticker reading *Silly boys, don't ya know Jeeps are for girls?* He hadn't noticed that yesterday, being stuck on the imaginative license plate instead. So, this must be Storm's vehicle of choice. It fit her better than the subcompact would have.

Stuffing the paper bag of borrowed clothes under his arm, he headed for the house. Rounding the SUV, he pulled up short, the breath escaping his lungs like a flat tire.

Storm Diana was draped over a shiny, black-and-chrome motorcycle, tinkering with something on what he assumed was the engine with some tool in her hand. She could have been a Roman goddess. Her blue jeans, faded and frayed in all the right places, must have been put on this morning with a paintbrush. Her sloppy jersey T-shirt was the exact contrast to the jeans; yet it blended well with the ponytail swinging at her shoulders, held in place by the ball cap. The shirt rode up her back just enough to flash him a glimpse of the black ink of her mystery tattoo. From this angle, he could only make out a block of ink.

She looked all boy and ultra-feminine. Quite a trick. Coughing down the lump forming in his throat, he waited for her to slowly lift her head and turn to face him. "Good morning," he greeted, trying to sound neutral—and failing. He sounded closer to a pubescent boy.

"Morning." She gave him a long look under her lashes while she twirled a long ratchet between her fingers.

He found the action oddly sexy and felt himself responding. His body tensed, and his heart hammered, mimicking the whirling sound of the ratchet. He worked to catch his breath. "Yours?" He nodded toward the motorcycle.

"Mine."

"I should think it would be hard to chase a storm while riding that."

She smiled.

He wondered if she was amused at his husky voice, or his tense stance. Did she have a clue how she affected him now?

"I store the bike here, store the SUV at the airport, and have another vehicle for most chasing I do. My team has it right now."

"In Oklahoma?"

She nodded, exchanging sockets on the ratchet. "Somewhere around there."

"So, you understand mechanics?" Not like he did. He paid someone to change the oil in his car, and he had only the most rudimentary knowledge of mechanical tools.

She paused, giving him a long look, then a tiny grin. "Not all girls are made up of sugar and spice."

No, some were made up of more combustible materials like dynamite, gasoline, and matches. What had the airships been powered by? Hydrogen? A reasonable comparison. Studying the woman before him, he saw truly little sugar but plenty of spice. Heated, fiery, hot spices to fuel that molten temper he knew lurked not far beneath her smiling exterior.

She replaced the new socket and picked up the original one, inserting it back in the ratchet.

Brody huffed a breath. She made her mind up just for the pleasure of changing it. Otherwise, she'd never bother.

"I know a few things a man should know."

"Like what?"

She grinned, tinkering with the engine. "How to change a flat. No time to wait for the auto club during a chase. How to hit a homerun. A girl's got to have a hobby." She threw out a flirty wink. "How to change oil, tow a trailer, and shoot a gun."

Her coy wink stole his breath again. Personally, he felt trusting her with a weapon of any kind was just reckless. Wisely, he refrained from telling her.

"I also know how to catch a fish and clean it for dinner. But Mama or Raine have to cook it." She grinned at the confession. Finally, she set the tools aside and stood, brushing her palms along the length of faded denim. "And how to know what love is." She approached him, giving his outfit of pressed khakis and oxford a long look. "You should have kept Winter's jeans and sweater. They looked better on you."

Taken aback by her sudden change, he shifted the bag and mentally reminded himself to breathe. "What's wrong with how I look?"

"Too uptight." She lifted her shoulder. "Do you ever relax, Brody McGee?"

The way his full name rolled off her tongue sent shivers over his spine and curled his toes. Her eyes were blue today, mirroring the skies above them. Calmer seas, he supposed. How long would it last? "Of course, I do. I'm calm now." He winced, thinking of her *KEEP CALM* license plate.

She laughed, lifting her head back. Her hands went to her belly, splaying her fingers. "Sure you are."

Irritation arose, pushing past the heat in his spine and toes. He took a step closer, taking in the sweet smell of maple syrup on her breath as she faced him squarely. Fearlessly. He just barely resisted the urge to lift a finger to her face. He wondered what it took to put fear in her eyes. A whole lot, he would bet. Sugar and spice? No, this woman was made up of guts and wanderlust. "And just what makes you think you are qualified to decide if I ever relax or not? Before you accosted me, three times mind you, we've never known each other. We had never met."

"But we do now," she maintained sweetly. "I know you like fruit-flavored bubble gum."

He frowned at her tart smile, his hands curling into fists around the bag of clothing. "That was my last stick, you know."

"What's the real reason you came to town?" She cocked her hip and rested one hand on it, while she looped her thumb through the belt loop of the other, and her eyes narrowed. "Because I don't think it's all it appears to be."

Stunned, he drew back at her challenge. His hands uncurled. He watched as her eyes grew large at his reaction and his lack of argument. He knew in his gut fear wasn't causing her eyes to round…his silent confirmation was. He felt busted, like a little kid caught stealing a cookie and then lying.

"Is Gallagher such a bad name for a Finn to marry?"

He shook his head, watching her eyes change from blue to green. Dread uncoiled in his chest. The color change was like watching a storm building up strength. How could he pacify her? He spread his hands out to disarm her. "It has nothing to do with the quality of the name. I know nothing of the merits of either name beyond my relationship with Calder."

"You're correct," she said levelly, taking a step in, closing the distance. Her brows narrowed.

Sweet maple scents formed a perfect opposition to her fiery anger.

"So you have no right to judge or decide who can be happy and marry just because you don't believe in happiness ever after."

Shocked at her fury, he blinked. She'd struck a little too close to the vein on that. The sweetness in her breath warred with the storminess of her eyes, clouding his mind. He needed another step back. "My personal thoughts on the institution of marriage have nothing to do with the situation at hand." Calder must have mentioned his sour view of marriage. Damn him. What hadn't he blabbed to these people?

She leaned closer, pleasing syrup on her breath and a dangerous light in her eye. "I don't believe you."

"Then don't," he said flatly, holding his ground, his own ire rising.

She stood rock solid, meeting his eye. Suddenly, without warning, she drew her hand back and let go, connecting her palm with his roughened cheek in a hard slap. "I warned you not to harm my family."

His jaw dropped, as did the bag of clothing, as his hand went to his throbbing cheek. "I can't believe you just slapped me, woman," he snarled, feeling heat burning his face and his eyes round in shock and pain.

"If you interfere with River and her wedding, you might get it again!" she promised, pinning him with a hard stare. "Or try to harm my family." She spun around and climbed on the bike, fired it up, and pushed it forward.

Amazed, astonished, and offended, Brody stood with his palm gingerly resting against the heated skin of his cheek.

She gunned the bike and tore out of the driveway.

Heated rage poured over him, and he bent over for

the bag. He raced across the sand to River's house and yanked at the door of his car. He tossed the clothing onto the front seat, cranked the engine, and backed out onto the road, taking off after the explosive redhead on the motorcycle.

He had no idea what he would do when he caught her, but he fully intended to make her pay for the stinging pain in his face. He'd light a match to her kerosene. Teeth gritted, he gripped the wheel of the rental car and turned onto the main street, heading for town.

He followed Storm as she raced through town, dodging cars and pedestrians, until she came to the drawbridge. Brody smiled in satisfaction at the sight and sound of clanging bells. The bridge was going up, and she would have to stop. He'd have her in just a minute. Off to the right, he saw the white mast of a boat, cruising out to sea. He slowed his car, ready to jump out and grab her once she stopped.

Suddenly he froze, forgetting to breathe as he watched her zip between the rails and lights, barely slowing down. She wouldn't? Would she? *Could she?* Fear had him out of his car. He heard her gun the throttle and lift off the inclining bridge, soaring through the air, above the water and empty space between the roads.

His heart stopped and then kick-started as he saw the rear end of the bike slide as she landed on the other side, momentarily losing control but quickly regaining it again.

Anger had him curling his fists and smashing them against the car as he watched her ride away, her red ponytail streaming in the wind.

Chapter Five

Storm landed and felt the rear of the bike slide, and she instinctively leaned into the slide, correcting the bike's direction. Straight once more, she gunned the throttle, racing south out of town.

Brody McGee! What was it with him? She seldom lost her temper to the point of slapping someone, no matter how badly they might deserve it. Now she had two things to apologize to him for—eventually. At this point, she might as well just start writing them down for one big delivery—eventually. When she could say it with meaning.

She knew he had followed her through town. Well, with the bridge up, he was halted for now. She gained some time to get away.

She didn't slow the bike until she had passed two more towns. The biting wind felt good on her face, reminding her of the stinging slap on her palm. Surely, it had stung him just as much to judge by the flash of surprise and recoiling pain in his blue eyes. Oh, her mom would pitch a fit if she found out about this latest infraction of good manners.

Bringing the bike to a stop in the town of South Tides, she parked it along the beachfront, facing the water. What would happen once she went back to town? She could not avoid him forever. Nor did she want to.

****

Brody parked his car at the marina where he had met Calder before. Was it only yesterday? Amazing but he felt like he'd been trapped in town for so much longer. First, he sat in the seat, fuming, his face burning, and wondering how long until the crazy woman returned. He used the car's vanity mirror to study his raw cheek. He planned to be here when she did return.

Finally, he realized she was in no great rush to return, so he got out and walked around. He tried to talk to the fishermen coming and going, but many just cast suspicious looks at him and went on their way. The town was not overly friendly. Naturally, they were wary of him, but honestly, he wasn't in the mood to figure out why. Was it so strange for someone to be parked at the marina? "I'm waiting to meet a woman," he explained to a few of them, if they dared to pause a moment. "Storm Gallagher."

Some simply shrugged and walked off, wishing him well. Others laughed openly in his face, adding insult to injury. Eventually, he stopped offering explanations.

Finally Calder phoned, saying he was taking a break from painting the living room and wanted to meet.

Brody declined, stating he was busy with something.

"Storm?" Calder simply guessed.

Brody huffed. "The crazy broad just jumped the bridge. On her motorcycle."

"I'm not surprised. Be glad she didn't take you along. Or dump you in the water again. Or worse. I've heard some stories about her." Calder's voice trailed off in a deep sigh.

Brody could easily picture him shaking his head in disbelief. His frustration mounting, Brody promised to call his partner once he set things straight with Storm.

Chuckling, Calder agreed, reminding him what time dinner was being served that evening.

"Funny, partner," Brody snapped, ending the call and returning to his wait. The longer he waited, the angrier he grew. That bold, brassy, fearless minx would surely pay when she crept back into town. Whenever the hell that proved to be.

He paced the length of sand, hands fisted into the pockets of his jacket, shoulders square and seething in anger. He watched the boats cruise into the marina and out to sea. Each time the horns blasted, he jumped. He glared at the birds circling and crying over his head, some grey, some brown, and some black-and-white. Others waded along the shore, dipping long beaks into the waves. They did not interest him. Back home, he had pigeons to contend with, and these were simply different, larger versions of pigeons.

Instead, his mind stayed on Storm and how his heart stopped as she sailed through the air, over the open water. He saw her lounging over that bike in her tight jeans looking like a centerfold. She was beautiful, and she knew it. Beautiful, fearless, and dangerous. From a distance, he heard a throaty rumble and loud pops. In his mind, he saw the centerfold version of Storm, with braids of red hair and beads framing her face.

"What are you doing here, boy?"

Spinning around, he spotted a weathered old man

approaching, carrying two buckets. His stomach swirled at the vile stench rising from the buckets. "I am waiting for someone. Storm Gallagher."

The old man smiled, showing off a few spaces where he was missing teeth. He set the buckets down and adjusted his cap. Finished, he picked the buckets back up. "Well, don't just stand there with your teeth in your mouth, boy," he said. "Come help me load the boat." He jerked his head back toward an ancient pickup truck. Brody suspected this was the source of the loud popping sounds moments ago.

"Little Storm will be along when she gets here. And when she does, you'll know it, boy." He shuffled away toward the bobbing board.

His amused smile added to Brody's annoyance. Brody blinked. What was with calling him *boy*? Teeth in his mouth? He self-consciously ran his tongue over his teeth. What?

Frown deepening, he stalked over to the truck and peered at the assorted buckets and nets and things in the back. The old guy expected him to lug it all over to some boat? Well, it wasn't like he had anything else to do—except wait on "Little" Storm to blow back into town. Grimly, he grabbed two handfuls of buckets and nets. His stomach muscles tightened as another wave of nausea gripped him. Fish, salt, and who knew what else rose to his nose, making him gag on the sour stench.

Oh yes, no doubt he would know when Storm arrived. And so would she. Because his own mood was growing like an approaching storm. This was going to be explosive.

****

The roar of a motorcycle roused Brody. He jerked

his head up, not aware he had fallen asleep behind the wheel. Hours had passed since he helped that old fisherman load his boat, but his anger had not cooled in the least.

Sure enough, a rider on a bike, with long hair flying beneath the ball cap was just crossing the bridge. At least, she was crossing it in a more conventional method this time. He flicked his headlights at her and climbed from the wheel, stretching as he watched her slow and turn his direction.

No helmet. He shook his head in disgust. He remembered the red ponytail streaming behind her. He assumed she'd somehow had a helmet on the bike and put it on. Evidently not. Didn't she know the dangers of riding one of those contraptions without a hard head covering? He checked the time. Where the hell had she been for over three hours? She set the kickstand and climbed off, taking a moment to stretch herself. The sight of that skintight denim hugging those lean legs made him swallow back a groan. His gut tightened as the jersey rode up to expose her navel and toned skin, and he caught a fleeting glimpse of black ink. Now was not the time to learn what her tattoo might be. He marched over, closing the distance between them in big strides. "What the hell was that fool stunt?"

She shrugged and pushed her windblown hair behind one ear. "No big deal."

"You think you're Evil Knievel's daughter or something?"

"I've jumped that bridge a few times. It's no big deal, so relax, Brody McGee."

Oh no, he wasn't going for that again. His face still twitched, reminding him. Grabbing her arm, he hauled her close, where he could still smell maple syrup sweet on her breath. She did not fight him; instead, she boldly met his glare. He'd hoped his anger would spike a pinch of fear into her, but apparently not. "And how many times has someone needed to pull you out of the water?"

She tossed him a pretty smile, one he imagined she meant to disarm him. "Not a single time. I always land where I want to." She boldly met his glare. "Is this where we see who the toughest and bravest is between us?" She tilted her head. "Do we eat worms? Or arm wrestle? What do you want to do?"

She didn't want to know what he wanted to do. If she kept goading him, she'd find out. "You are crazy," he declared, heat pouring over him at the lights dancing in her eyes. His anger stepped aside as a new primal emotion nudged it away.

She laughed, unfazed by his accusation. "Maybe. Maybe not. But who are you to decide that?"

Impulsively, he snatched her arm, bringing her face to meet his, capturing her hot and moist lips with his. Pressing hard, he took her breath away and felt immensely satisfied at the startled gasp and then her return probe. Barely keeping a thin hold on his anger, he held her, taking what breath she had, and made her taste his fury. Finally dizzy, he released only her lips, still holding both her arms gripped in his fists. "Woman," he declared, his voice husky. "That gives me every right."

Storm ran her tongue over her lips, already bruising from his demanding kiss. Her breathlessness matched his, and he suspected his eyes smoldered much like hers did.

Her chest rose and fell once.

He watched her; his breath held for her next reaction. He would love nothing better than to claim another kiss like that one.

"You kiss pretty well, Brody McGee."

Sparks ignited in her eyes as his name rolled off her tongue. She lifted her lips in a smirking grin and jutted her chin out, ready to defy him. Fresh heat dumped over him like embers. He tightened his grip on her arms, smiling at her slight cry. He sorted through his mind for names, discounting them quickly. Honey, sugar, sweetheart. No, none of those fit her. Those were all too sweet. She was spice, fiery spice, and all woman. Hot, demanding, infuriating woman.

"Storm Diana," he growled, finally settling on the straightforward answer. "You have no idea."

Crushing his lips to hers again, he felt the waves of desire sluicing over him. How explosive of a union would they prove to be? The weakness spreading over his body and tightness surrounding his chest begged him to find out—soon.

****

Storm helped her mom cook dinner. Tonight, it would just be her and her parents.

Raine had other commitments, and River said Calder needed some time with Brody to talk about their business back in Atlanta. River hinted she could pop in later for dessert to give the boys time alone.

As she stirred the bowl her mom had instructed her to mix, she wondered how Brody McGee would react if she popped in on their alone time. Storm figured it would be the perfect way to welcome Calder to the family, of course. And, if all else failed, she could say she was dropping by to apologize to Brody.

She smiled; her hands stilled over the mixing bowl. She had yet to apologize. After their exchange of kisses at the marina, it had slipped her mind. His anger had been a beautiful thing to experience, much like a slow-building storm. Just the memory was enough to take her breath away.

Once it finally reached its peak, it could be a great experience. The heat of his kiss and the iron of his grip had touched off sparks within her she had never felt from a man before. Her body's reaction was exciting. And just a tiny bit scary, like being in the bear cage of a storm. When you almost forget to breathe.

"Storm!" Muriel exclaimed, entering the kitchen. "Mind what you are doing, girl."

Looking down, she flushed at the wet ingredients spilling over the counter and onto the floor. "Oops, sorry, Mom," Storm apologized as she righted the bowl and then reached for some paper towels.

"Wool gathering again?" Muriel wadded her apron and sopped at the spill on the counter.

"Yeah, guess so." Storm knelt, scrubbing the mess on the floor. Her face had to be as red as her sister's nails.

With the mess cleaned, Muriel surveyed the damage. "Now dinner will be delayed while you start over again. I'll go tell your father."

About to apologize again, and even offer to explain the delay herself to her dad, Storm was brought up short as her mother patted her cheek.

"Storm, darling, the trouble with doing nothing is that it's too difficult to tell when you are finished." With that, she walked from the room.

Heat still touching her face, she returned to measuring and mixing, this time pulling her thoughts off the combined excitement of she and Brody and onto the meal ahead. Her mother would not be so forgiving a second time around.

Time enough later to get back to Brody McGee. She had a strong suspicion he wasn't going anywhere soon.

****

"We need to discuss us leaving town," Brody tried to keep his voice low. "Going back home." He studied Calder's change of expression as they sat in the backyard and Calder studied a book of paint swatches River had given him.

Calder looked up from the samples, his right index finger resting on one particular square. He shook his head. "Buddy, there is nothing to discuss. I'm marrying River and staying here for a while. The only time I plan to return to Atlanta in the immediate future, before the wedding, is whenever I can get River away to go with me, if I can get her to stop obsessing over painting the house."

He grinned like a happy fool as he tapped the blue square beneath his fingertip.

"I need to return the rental car at the airport, pack some things at the condo, and check on a few things at the firm," Calder continued. "I want River to see the local sights, and we'll fly back home to finish organizing the wedding." He paused, taking a breath, and closing the paint sample book. "I just need her to free up enough time to do all that. Plus we have that court hearing next week." He looked outside, his expression softening. "I want to marry River and watch our kids grow up, running along that shore." He looked back at Brody. "Now, we can discuss anything else."

Brody fought to bite back his grimace and swallow his groan of impatience. This was not going to be easy. He gave a slight shake of his head in response to Calder. His buddy grinned, and Brody would bet the firm he figured he'd just upended him. Well, Calder Finn didn't know him well if he thought this matter was over. He just needed to rethink things over. Then he'd be better prepared the next time.

****

Their dinner was done, and River was cleaning up. Brody and Calder were on the back porch, watching the waves and drinking beer. Brody was trying his best to figure this mess out. Images of airbrushed redheads continued to infiltrate his mind, but he stubbornly latched on to the more pressing matter of his partner.

He took a swig of beer and looked at the nearly barren shore. What would they be doing right now if they were back home in Atlanta? At seven o'clock on a Wednesday night? Certainly not this. "So you were raised here?" He needed something to say as his mind was a total blank as far as a new plan. He wished he'd tossed Calder in the car that first moment at the marina. Before he could meet that redhead again. Before he could see for himself how much Calder liked it here. In time, he would have forgiven him for what would have amounted to a kidnapping. Too late, a plan formed in his mind. He swallowed an irritated breath because he was thinking up plans too late to use them now. What was the matter with him?

"Yeah."

"It's really small." Brody said the first thing that

popped into the empty space of his mind.

"Yeah." Calder took another pull on his drink. "So, what happened with you and Storm today?"

"Nothing. We had a disagreement. She's crazy."

Calder grinned. "Cordell might just say she's only high strung."

Brody snorted, almost dropping his drink. "High strung," he repeated. "That's putting it mildly." Looking at Calder, he realized, belatedly, he'd just played into his friend's hand. "Look," he said, raking a hand through his hair in mounting frustration, both at Calder and Storm. And himself. "I personally don't care who you marry, if you marry, where you marry, or any of that. If you want to sign on the dotted line with some woman, that's great. You know I'll cover your back the whole way. But, Calder, man, we have the firm to think about. Just how long do you think you can stay here and expect it to keep on running itself? Matt is going to qualify for early retirement if we don't return soon."

Calder gave him a maddening grin, probably to both egg on his irritation and just being Calder.

"I didn't expect you to come running up here so soon, though I'm glad you're here. I expected you to come for the wedding and, in the meantime, keep the firm going without me." He took a pull on his beer, then set it down and looked out to the shore. "Hadn't we both agreed the firm needed to run indefinitely with just one of us at the helm? As one of those in case plans of yours?" He cut a glance over at Brody.

Yes, his ever-famous contingency plans in case something had happened to either of them. Or both. He shook his head. "I hadn't intended on you testing the resiliency of the plan already."

Calder chuckled. "So, go back to Atlanta if it worries you so much. Come back for the wedding. I'll keep in better touch, promise. It's easier now that I'm not in jail."

He'd thought about it. Brody still had a hard time picturing Calder in jail. He also noted how he had said "Atlanta" and not "home." Was it possible he already considering this sandy desolation of wind and water to be his home again? What was left in Atlanta for him besides their firm and him?

In a sobering reality check, he realized they both lived their lives around their business and each other. A cold shudder raced over him, and he scrubbed his arms, wishing it was just the salt air. "So what's the deal with old man Gallagher?" Brody changed gears again. "You two seemed pretty chummy last night."

"He likes it when I join him for drinks and conversation after dinner. I think he views me as a substitute for Winter."

That seemed reasonable enough. And it might be some form of substitute for what Calder never had with his father, as well.

River came out onto the porch, both dogs at her feet.

Immediately, the white terrier went to Calder, paw lifted to his knee.

"I'll take the dogs for a walk and then go see Storm and Mom and Dad." River wrapped her arms around Calder's neck and moving in for a quick nip behind his ear.

Brody looked away, watching the black dog daintily pick her way down the wooden steps. River's giggle sent shivers crawling down his spine, and he wondered if Storm would giggle like that.

Probably not, she was more the type to bodily throw a man down and then give out a lusty, mighty conquering battle cry of an Amazon warrior woman, instead. And the man she was going to surmount had better just lie there and enjoy it, or else.

Suddenly Brody squirmed, yanking his thoughts to the mint-scented air. It did little to drive the warmth from his body. So preoccupied with thoughts of savage, red-haired Amazon women and throaty battle cries, he barely heard River as she took the dogs down to the beach.

"Buddy, you look like you were miles away. Dreaming?" Calder snapped his fingers in front of Brody. "You want me to go with River and leave you alone, with whoever else is in there with you?"

Heat filled Brody's face, and horror filled his mind. Coughing, he shook his head. "No, we need to talk more. Stay here."

Calder sighed, grinning as he settled back in the chair. "I never thought I'd live to see that kind of look on your face."

That's okay. Brody didn't think he'd ever live to experience the varied emotions and feelings flitting through him and teasing his mind. But he refused to reply to Calder's goad.

Calder sighed. "Okay, what else is on your mind?"

"The firm. We must make some decisions whether you like it or not." Business. He could handle talking about business a whole lot easier than dealing with the thoughts Storm Diana caused. "We owe that to Matt and the others, not to mention our clients." Work was a safer topic.

****

On the next day, Brody and Calder were tricked into running errands for River. Brody wasn't sure how it exactly happened, but he and Calder found themselves sitting in Muriel Gallagher's living room, listening to her wax on about the twins.

"Winter was supposed to be born first; you know." Muriel handed over glasses of lemonade to Calder and Brody.

The whole thing started with River watering a plant with white flowers, fondly stroking the leaves.

He entered the room and caught her admiring it as she poured the water around it. Hearing him, she looked up, sniffing. She plucked a tissue from the nearby box and dabbed her eyes. "This belonged to Frank," she told him as she gently rubbed her finger along the new petals.

"It's pretty." Not that he knew much about flowers.

"He'd received it once his cancer diagnosis became known in town, and I couldn't bear to leave it behind at the empty house."

"You still miss him?" he guessed, hands going to his pockets. Normally crying woman made him uncomfortable and look for the exit sign. Being with River as she cried was unsettling but not uncomfortable. He just had no idea how to comfort her. So he stood, hands in his pockets, listening to her.

"Yes, I do. Every day." She ran a fingertip along the slender buds, blinking rapidly. "That Jordan woman damaged it when she ransacked his house, but with some TLC, it's coming around. These are the first new buds." She smiled a tight-lipped grin. "And as much as I miss Frank, I feel lucky to be marrying his son."

Something stabbed Brody's chest. Her vulnerable side took him aback, and he struggled to find words of comfort or affirmation. He glanced at Calder, who walked up, lifted her hair, and nuzzled the back of her neck. Brody expected them to turn it into a Public Display of Affection event.

Instead, River gripped Calder's hand and nodded, sniffing again. Then, mustering a smile, she smoothed her hair and went on to talk about how she had to go to Watercolors, which was what she called her property development company, and would they mind going to just a couple places for her?

Exchanging shrugs, he and Calder agreed and somehow were now delivering bagged items to Muriel in exchange for refreshing sweet lemonade. One of many errands on River's list. Their list of chores had afforded Brody a full view of the town, which appeared to be one aged nautical building after another, full of seaside-sounding names and signs. Even some of the houses, most of which were up on stilts, bore catchy, beach-themed name plaques or road signs. Soon, he and Calder were back at Finn Summit, with Muriel and sweet tea. And stories of Storm and Winter.

"Really?" Calder commented. "What happened? They're twins."

Muriel smiled fondly as she took a seat in the living room. "Well, Winter had been lined up first for a couple days already, all poised to be the first one out into the world. The ultrasound images had been very clear about that. Their due date was almost here, and we were having a terrible blizzard, worse in probably one hundred years, and we could not get to the hospital. Lola Finn, your mama, Calder, came over to assist with the delivery. Lola had been my friend for more years than I recall.

"At that last moment, Storm suddenly pushed Winter back, out of the way, and she dashed right out the womb first. They have been that way ever since. You should have heard her first cries of anger."

Brody did not doubt it. He could picture her doing something just like that. He knew nothing of babies being born, and whether her story was a hundred percent accurate or not, but it sure sounded like something Storm would do. He took another drink of lemonade, its sweetness tempered by the tang of lemon. "So, where is Storm at?" He looked around, hoping to see her.

"She and her daddy have gone off down the beach, fishing for dinner. If I know those two, they'll grow bored, empty-handed, and end up at the local fish market, instead."

Yes, Brody could see that, too. She knew how to catch a fish, as long as it came from the local fish market, already trapped. Disappointment sliced through him with the realization she was not going to bump into him. Already, their glasses were about empty, and they were out of excuses to stay longer. And he was about to elbow Calder, hard, if he gave him one more pointed grin like that. "That was a wonderful story and thank you for the lemonade." He deposited his glass on the counter and reached over to crowd Calder. "But we probably should get going on the list of errands we have."

"Why the rush?" Calder put his sunglasses on as they entered the rental car. "We've got plenty of time."

"You're the one who wanted to finish this list up,

from your fiancée, by lunchtime," Brody reminded, wondering where the bit of hostility came from bubbling up within him. "So, let's get cracking." He slid his own dark sunglasses on, jutted his chin out, and waited for Calder to start the car.

Calder chuckled and turned the car over. "Oh, this could get very entertaining."

Brody snorted. "For you, maybe."

Calder drove him around the entire town, not that it was all that large to begin with. Every storefront was weathered and nautical, most bearing imaginative maritime names. Worn wooden floors squeaked in most where they stopped to visit. The people were reserved but friendly. Calder introduced him, but he would fail a test if he were to recall who was who.

In most cases, Calder was the landlord, checking on the tenants, the buildings, or both, and delivering letters from River. "River is the expert," Calder explained though Brody hadn't asked. "I'm still figuring it all out."

Based on what Brody observed, once his partner figured it all out, he would see he owned a sizeable portion of a small seaside town full of old buildings and reserved people. Would he still want to stay then?

The last stop was Watercolors, to report everything was completed. They walked through the front door, and Brody waved at River.

She looked up from reviewing some papers with an older, heavyset woman with brown hair twisted in a bun. River smiled but quickly stepped into Calder's open embrace.

"Hello, I'm Brody McGee, his partner," Brody introduced himself to the secretary since the young lovers were otherwise too busy—again.

"Pleased. I'm Daphne." She gave him a quick study before offering him a smile. "You are not a local."

"No. I have never been here before. I just came to town for…" His response trailed off as he looked at Calder, still locked in an embrace with River.

"You don't have the accent. I also never had you in any of my classes."

"Classes?" Calder perked up as he pulled his mouth off River's neck. "You taught classes?"

"For twenty-five years before I retired and started working for River."

"Daphne?" Calder repeated as he stared at her face. "Mrs. Kingston?" His voice was barely above a whisper.

Brody watched with rapt attention at the doom drifting down over his partner's face.

She nodded silently; her lips pursed together.

Calder smacked a hand to his forehead and looked over at Brody. "Now I see! No wonder Daphne has never liked me. I hated every single class she taught, and I was quite possibly one of her worst, if not more willful, students. I personally carried many letters home to my parents from her for several years, outlining my wild behaviors of the week."

River chuckled and wrapped her arms around Calder's neck. "I thought you knew all along who Daphne was. She always made her thoughts about you known to me. And I will still marry you." She gave another snicker of amusement. "You won't believe the stories I have heard."

"I can just imagine," Calder muttered thickly.

Brody watched the exchange that so clearly yelled "small town" and found it utterly fascinating. He rubbed his chin, and he realized what a unique situation he was standing in. The advantage of being an outsider, the people would only know what Calder might have shared. He was largely a man of unknowns. His life prior to joining Calder in college is a complete mystery to everyone. He could never expect surprises like Calder just walked into. However amusing this situation was, he didn't care to be caught in a similar one.

And this small-town slice of life also afforded him a bird's eye view of Storm's life. These were the people who knew her best, from when she was a small child to growing up and leaping motorcycles over rising drawbridges and everything in between.

Maybe, just maybe, he needed to test the plan of leaving the firm to run itself for a while longer, with Matt at the helm. He could go ahead and stay for a bit. He might learn a lot more than he originally thought was possible. Yes, he could just make a couple calls, check in with some members of the staff, make sure everything was still running smoothly, and stay in town to see what was going to unfold.

He had a strong hunch that airbrushed, crazy redhead was going to stick around, too. He could poke around and easily see what he could learn about her exploits. He would just bet Mrs. Daphne Kingston would have a story or two to share from Storm's school days. Probably a whole bunch of them.

He eyed her half-empty coffee mug sitting on the corner of the desk and would have bet that for the price of a couple of cups of coffee, he would glean a lot of interesting academic information about Storm. A small town like this had to have lots of people like Daphne who could each contribute a few stories of their own, slowly completing the puzzle. Just like the people he had met today who'd lived here for most or all of Storm's life.

A new plan formed in his mind. Finally, he might have landed upon something that could work.

Chapter Six

Brody adjusted the collar of his polo shirt and watched River tap her foot. A smile tugged on his lips, and he looked away, pretending to be interested in an abstract orchid painting on her wall. He and River were waiting for Calder so they could go out to dinner at some restaurant in town. He'd found himself anxious, hoping Storm might stop in, but River had shrugged and said no one ever knew with her. He was getting the impression Storm did what Storm wanted to do, when she wanted to do it. She had her own timetable. She—

"I think it's great you are able to stay in town longer, Brody," River said. "For a little while there, the way you were talking, I thought you were leaving us soon."

He shook his head. "No, I just needed to get all the appropriate knowledge in order to make the correct decision." He jerked a thumb at Calder. "This guy here is bad for not providing all the accurate information sometimes. Then it takes a search party to uncover it all." That comment was a tiny stretch of the truth, but he pacified himself by saying it wasn't too much. And it was part of his new plan.

"Don't I know it." River swirled her hands in the air to highlight her point. "Why, you would not believe what happened just a couple days ago. Right before you arrived in town. He—"

Calder noisily cleared his throat, staring at the two of them. "If you are both done browbeating my many faults, can we please leave now? I am starving."

Brody glanced at River. Maybe it did seem like they did tend to pick on Calder just a little. He shot his partner a smile. "Well, if you didn't have so many faults for us to browbeat, we'd have to sing your praises, instead."

"Apparently that would be a short conversation," Calder muttered darkly. "Are you ready?"

"Sure, we can always pick this conversation back up later," Brody teased, slapping Calder on his way out.

"One thing you have never answered to my satisfaction, partner, is why did you come to town, but you never managed to pack your tux or any formal wear?"

Because attending a wedding never factored into his plans for this trip, but he'd rather die than tell Calder the truth. He grinned and lifted his shoulder in a shrug. "You know how it is."

"I know how you are. You're normally a better planner."

"And you're normally a better communicator."

River watched their exchange, a slow grin spreading over her lips. "You know, guys, sometimes I get tempted to think you two barely tolerate each other. Between Brody's irritable snapping and Calder's sarcastic droll, I wonder how you two can stay partners." She paused to hug Calder. "But now, I am beginning to see it as more of a close brotherhood, instead, layered with fond teasing and good-natured bantering. You have the same familiar ease with each other that I have with my sisters, especially Raine. It is really something to see that same kind of bond from this side looking in."

Brody wasn't sure what to say. He'd just taken his relationship with Calder at face value, and he'd never dissected it deeper than it seemed. He glanced at Calder and lifted one eyebrow in silent question.

Calder did the same, and then pulled River in for a kiss. "Trust my future bride to see our lives like that." Before River could reply, Calder puckered up and planted a huge kiss on her lips, making her giggle.

Brody studied the wall while the two kissed. He hummed quietly as their smooches intensified.

Finally, they broke apart, and Calder punched Brody in the shoulder. "Ready?" he asked, a huge smile cutting his face.

Brody noticed how Calder's hand quickly slipped over River's. He swallowed a lump as he led the way outside. "So, tell me more about this place we're going to," Brody asked once they made it to the car "What If?"

Calder shrugged and started the car. "The land and building are part of our town holdings. The restaurant is new, only about two years old. It is quite trendy, considering the persona of the town." He cast a fast look at River before continuing. "They have shown a slow, steady profit each year. The tenants of the restaurant are younger than most of the town's population, but I have not had time to sit down and meet individually with them."

"Is that something you plan to do?" Brody tilted his head to one side. This was something they had talked about doing in Atlanta but had never actually started. Once they signed the client and their property, all the attention shifted to managing the real estate, and not dealing much one-on-one with the clients. He and Calder had discussed it and thought routine sit-downs would help open doors and promote good will. They'd gotten as far as scheduling a few clients and sending their more-seasoned team members to meet.

"Yes, with each tenant, starting with the business ones. So far, I have had meetings with only three." He blew out a sigh. "It's been a slow process, but it will be worth it. Reading portfolio reports only tells you so much."

Brody rubbed his chin thoughtfully, scratching his beard. "True. There is no substitute for personal groundwork" He turned to River. "Back home, we always met with new clients, but never reconnected unless a problem arose. We'd thought about starting regular meetings with established clients, to ensure things were going smoothly. It's been slow to get off the ground." Yet here, Calder was implementing their plan in his town.

She nodded. "Of course. I have always done the same here for Frank's holdings and all my client's holdings. Can't just sit in an office all day pushing numbers around."

"Atlanta isn't my home anymore, buddy," Calder pointed out tightly, failing to meet his gaze.

Brody cringed, and something lurched in his stomach. How could he convince Calder to return to Atlanta? How could he explain their lives were there? Maybe he could convince River to leave her family and life here to join them there? But then he'd never see Storm again.

Something slithered over him, burning hot at first,

and then cold. Before he could analyze the reaction, Calder parked the car. River and Calder swung their doors open. Outside, the building looked much the same as the rest of the Sweetwater Harbor marine design, except the sign was bright and fresh, with a fun font reading simply *What If?*

What if, indeed.

Inside the restaurant, they found good seats near the windows overlooking the harbor and ordered their meals and a bottle of wine to share. Brody opted for the butter burger and fries while Calder and River each had a different fish and chips meal. Conversations alternated between business discussions, process comparisons, and nostalgic banter. Brody looked around at the brightly painted walls, polished hardwood floors, and strategically placed mirrors. The place lacked the marine aged atmosphere of the other buildings he'd seen so far, and the contemporary background music lent a modern vibe.

"Oh, hey look!" A big smile crossed River's face, and she waved joyfully at the entrance.

Looking up, Brody nearly gagged on the last bite of his butter bun. He reached for the wineglass to quickly wash it down.

Calder pushed out two seats.

"We didn't know you guys were here," Raine said as she and Storm took the seats.

"It's more of a business dinner." River shrugged at Brody and Calder. "These two are as exciting as a board meeting."

"And what would you know about board meetings?" Calder shot back, smiling as he captured her hand in his.

"You would be surprised." She dismissed his remark and turned back to her sisters. "So what brings you here?"

"Just something different. We had dinner already, and Stormie here"—Raine jerked a thumb at her sister—"is already tired of being with Mom and Dad."

"That is not true!" Storm protested. "I was bored to tears with whatever show they had on the television." She rolled her eyes. "It was in black and white!"

The sisters shared a laugh.

Brody studied the trio. A lethal package, taken either individually or as a threesome set. He silently wished Calder well with handling River. Seemed like playing with lit sticks of dynamite to him.

"Ohh, I love this song," River exclaimed suddenly, whirling to grab Calder's hand. "Come on, honey. Let's dance."

Before he could protest, he was dragged out onto the floor, shooting Brody a satisfied smile as he swept River into his arms. Brody could tell River unquestionably had his partner tied around her little finger. And that made it much harder to pry him away and return home.

"I see a friend of mine. See you in a bit." Raine excused herself and joined a small group across the room.

Storm blew out a long sigh, resting her chin on her upturned palms. "That just leaves us. Care to dance?" She reached for his wineglass, helping herself.

The fingers on her other hand trailed along his right hand, sending electricity racing up his arms.

"Do you dance, Brody McGee?" She replaced the glass, and gave him a pouty smile.

He almost laughed. This was going to be like spinning around a packed room with a live bomb, without the benefit of protective gear. And Storm lived to pull that pin and set it off, to borrow from a phrase Cordell had said. And…he couldn't think of anything else he would rather do right then.

He extended a hand, pulling her up. "Of course. We must take a twirl or two around." If for no other reason than to show off those airbrushed-on jeans, faded and ripped in all the right places. They set his mind to wandering in all sorts of directions. He led her onto the floor and rested his hands along the exposed skin beneath her cropped white sweater. She was soft, yet strong in his arms. Her scents of fruit and spice swirled around him, making him light-headed. Her hair was loose, and as she tipped her head back to meet his face, it fell to his fingertips where he could wrap a couple curling tendrils around his fingers.

She looped her arms around his neck, keeping him close.

Would she boldly kiss him again, like she had at the airport? A knot formed in his stomach. If she didn't, should he? Umm, what if indeed. His tongue swelled just thinking about her explosive, wet kiss. "So, jump any more drawbridges lately?" he asked as they fell into step with the music and natural step with each other.

She laughed, rich and a pleasant melody. "No, not lately."

Glancing down, he noticed her tattoo playing peekaboo in the small of her back. He tried to identify it. Black ink danced in the mirrored light, dipping, and disappearing beneath her waistband. Curious, he tried to follow it, like focusing on a moving target. Finally, he gave up, switching his full attention to her eyes instead. Bluer today, caught in the overhead lights of the dance floor, reflecting amusement as she laughed.

"You dance well. For a city boy."

"And you dance well yourself. For a storm chaser."

She tilted her head to the side, her lips thinning into a thoughtful line. "Does my profession bother you?"

"I wouldn't say it bothers me. I would more accurately say I don't understand it."

She pulled him even closer, bridging the narrow gap that had been there.

He could smell spiced cider on her breath and see the moist glossiness of her lipstick. Familiar heat poured over him as he remembered the taste of those searing lips.

Suddenly, she grabbed him by the hair on the back of his head, fisting the cropped hair, and pushed her lips to his, plunging her tongue into his mouth.

Startled, he recovered quickly, tasting her, and asking for more. He now grabbed the hair that had been twined around his fingers a second ago as he closed the final tiny bit of distance between them. He felt her chest crush against his. Closing his eyes, he prepared to sweep over her, to demand more, because he knew she had it in reserves.

Without warning, she stopped, withdrawing.

The action left him empty and adrift. Licking her lips, she gave him another satisfied smile, much like that first smile as she departed the airplane. When she had left him speechless and blown away.

"That is like storm chasing, Brody. Fast, pleasurable, and unexpected sometimes, stealing your breath. You don't always have to understand it. But it sure helps when you do. It's more important you just live it."

Breathless, he took her back into his arms, at a loss for words.

She cut him a laugh, moving away as the song ended. She took his hand and led away from where the others were already regrouping.

Wordlessly, he followed her out to the covered deck.

She grabbed hold of the railing and spun around to face him.

"You are a hard person to figure out, Storm Diana."

She tossed her hair back, giggling. "I am not a one-dimensional broad. I have my own beat, my own drummer, and my own rhythm." She gave him a serious look, her eyes narrowed, lips thinned, shoulders back, and hip cocked to the side. She rested one hand on the hip for good measure. "I'm complicated. I am more than what meets the eye. So, why bother trying?"

Why indeed? Devil of a good question. And every word she spoke he knew to be true. "Because it is what I do," he finally said. "Understand and plan things."

She leveled a look at him. "Not everything is meant to be understood and catalogued into tidy little cubbyholes. Or everyone. Some things and some people are just meant to be enjoyed for what they are."

And here, he thought, was a woman who knew completely how to enjoy life moment by moment, seizing what she chose from it, giving back only what she wanted, and living it all on her terms. For one fleeting moment, as he watched her swing around the pole as innocent and free as a schoolgirl, he envied her.

But he had his facts and figures. While maybe it was not as exciting as her chosen path, he knew safety existed in data. So, what was there to be envious of?

She looked out at the sky, smiling, as she reached her upturned palm out to capture the first droplets of rain. "Brody, come on. Let's go out there." She beckoned him out beyond the steps, her other hand reaching for him.

"No way." He shook his head. "It's raining." Well, it was going to rain in just a minute. Or two. Close enough.

She chuckled, turning back again. "These are just playful clouds. Come on out with me."

"Playful clouds?" Was that another of her own technological terms River had said she was prone to come up with?

"You're not scared, are you?" she challenged.

"Of course not." Scared. Of water falling from the sky? Pride had him stepping to the edge of the deck, ready to tread down. A crack of lightning snapped, and he withdrew a space, reaching for her hand as he retreated. "Get up here. You'll get blown away."

"Relax, it's miles away."

He reached for her arm, missing again. He frowned. "It's lightning. How can you possibly know where it's at?" She favored him with another smile, one indicating he might be stupid, before she turned back to spread her arms wide in the rain.

She spun in a circle, laughing at the droplets. "It's barely anything, Brody McGee. Just nimbostratus clouds." She stopped and looked at him. "This is just a little bit of rain." She lifted her hair, now wet, and turned her face up to the sky, turning into another circle as she giggled. "A baby shower."

He huffed, not appreciating the reference, however slight. It only served to remind him of what might happen with his business partner. With marriage came wives, and with wives came babies. While he liked both fine enough, they had not been part of the plan when he and Calder formed their firm. Somehow, the possibility either one of them might fall in love and marry had never been equated into their business plans. And being in another town in another state certainly never had. In his heart, he just assumed he and Calder would always be in Atlanta. Did that make him naïve? Stupid? Yet, now here it was, the very real fact pushing itself through.

"It's glorious, Brody. Come on out here and feel it."

He stood on the deck, arms folded over his chest, watching her. She reminded him of the young girls playing in mud puddles in their galoshes he used to see when he lived in Boston. Such contrasts, he decided, unable to avoid cataloguing her. This was the same woman who could slap his face and jump a drawbridge on a motorcycle and push him bodily into the ocean.

She could also be brave enough to pick him out as a stranger in a crowded airport terminal and physically accost him with wet kisses. She was also spinning and dancing and laughing in the rain like a child on her way home from school.

Her facets seemed to have no end. Now, why did that revelation please him so?

The lightning crack drew his gaze over the water, but he also noticed she never bothered to look. Was anything ever serious to her? But, compared to what she might have seen in her line of work, this was nothing more than a mere passing shower. A little bit of rain. A baby shower. He exhaled deeply.

She raised her arms up again, lifting her hair off her shoulders and turning in another circle. Her cropped sweater rode up. A wicked grin teased her lips.

Brody swallowed, watching her slowly spin, mesmerized by her toned, flat belly and the blocky tattoo peeking back as it played hide and seek. Tornado? Tasmanian Devil? Both were appropriate She packed as much punch as both. He heaved a sigh and dropped a hand to splay over his chest. "Woman, you are hard on the heart."

She stepped up to the top step, hand curled around the railing. She rocked back on her heels and pulled at her bottom lip. Then she smiled. "I could give you mouth to mouth."

"I just bet you would." For one fleeting minute, his mind grabbed the image her suggestion made. He well remembered her sweet kiss on those pouty lips. His breath caught at the mischievous light glimmering in her eye. She ran her tongue over her upper lip and he inhaled, sucking down a groan.

This woman, fearless and flirty, was going to be the death of him!

****

"Mom wants to go into Lady Beth this week to find a dress," River said. "We can probably find all our dresses there." She ran her finger down the list in her notebook. She glanced over to Storm and then looked around Storm's bedroom where they sat on the floor opposite each other.

Once upon a time, they shared this room. She even

remembered the grey tape they'd laid down in the middle to divide the space when they were about thirteen and fifteen and seemed to squabble over everything. She exhaled a breath. How things changed over the years, including their relationship. "Now, Raine's got all the food and cake under control, of course."

"Naturally." Storm idly tossed the baseball up, catching it only to flip it up again.

River threw her a frown. "You could be helping me, you know," she muttered. "I still don't have a clue where to hold this at."

Storm laughed, still chucking and catching the ball. "Believe me, sis, I am helping you. If I were to touch any part of your wedding plans, it would all crumble down like a house of cards."

River considered that. It was probably true. Storm was no planner or organizer. She only planned her next move about three or four seconds before she acted upon it. She'd long ago lost track of how much trouble Storm—and Winter—got into as kids.

"Hey, I like him, don't get me wrong. Just because I'm not being all hands on here, don't think I don't like him."

Again, River contemplated that, slowly breaking into a grin. "Calder? Or Brody? Because last night, it looked an awful lot like you mean Brody."

Storm caught the ball, holding it, and deftly wrapping her fingers around its circumference. "I had been referring to Calder, your intended," she replied smartly. "Though Brody certainly has his good traits, as well." She grinned. "Oh, does he ever have them. Sis, the more time I spend around Brody, the more good and bad traits I can find."

River threw a pen at her. "You remind me of the Cheshire Cat. And I bet you like all the guys…good and especially the bad ones, right?"

"You know, there is this old saying about daughters marrying men who are like their father." Heat filled her face. "Calder doesn't seem anything like Daddy."

River paused, closing her notebook as she realized Storm was avoiding the topic again. She could change conversations like the wind. Especially when she had something to hide. "No, he isn't much like Daddy. But he is the son of the man I did have as a second father. That's pretty close."

Storm tilted her head. "That's true. I was never as close to Frank and like-minded as you were. But if Calder is half the man his dad was, I guess you're getting a prime man."

Opening her notebook, River smiled. "I happen to think I am getting a prime man. Now, we need to figure out where to have this ceremony. Come on and give me some suggestions." She took the pen back from Storm and stretched her legs out to tap Storm's feet with her own. They shared a smile.

****

Storm closed her eyes, clutching the baseball to her chest, letting her mind drift. She'd long ago accepted the fact she would never marry. She was too busy chasing and spread too far to the winds, as her mom and dad often called it. But if she were to ever do anything as insane as marry a man, where would she want the ceremony to be?

She'd been fortunate to see so much of the world,

so much more than her sisters, surpassed perhaps only by her brother. She knew of beautiful and wonderful places that would be perfect for a wedding. That River only knew Sweetwater Harbor seemed almost sad. Why, getting her and Mom to go all the way to Lady Beth for dress shopping was, in their own way, a huge ordeal. She smiled. To her, traveling to Lady Beth was just leaving town. To them, going away probably seemed more like the ends of the earth.

Whereas she left town for other states, other countries on occasion, and pursued life's anger. Her work was important, and she evidently became a target to someone. And wasn't it a great convenience she crossed paths with Brody at the airport? What if they hadn't met? She could not imagine selecting another person for her distraction. No, her initial assumption was correct—he was perfect.

"What's that smile for?" River looked up from her notes.

"I'm thinking. You asked where a good place is to be married, so I'm picking a good spot." She lifted one eye and studied River. "Is Colorado too far?"

"Uh, yeah, I think so. Can we please at least stick to North Carolina?"

"Fine. NC, it is." She wriggled into a comfortable position and rested her hands on her knees.

"You're not gonna start some mediation chant thing, are you?"

"Seriously, River, if you don't shut up, I'll never think of a place."

River grinned. "You know, Storm, for someone who lives for thrills and by split-second decisions, you can't seem to answer a straight and simple question."

Storm lifted one eyebrow, glared at her sister, blew out a huff of air, and folded her hands in front of her. "Okay, where could I see myself getting married? What location of so many stands out, with me decked in white and a veil—that does not come from Lady Beth, by the way—and with decorations and flowers and me standing next to a man dressed in a tux and bow tie?"

"That is the question."

****

River watched, growing just a touch impatient, as Storm ran her tongue over her lips and hummed. She had the Buddha look going. "Storm?"

"Oh, all right. I have several favorite regions and spots in mind, places I have been. Interestingly, they are mostly alongside places I've chased and seen nature's temper tantrum. I think it would be lovely to go back for my own wedding and see how nature and the people rebuilt. It would be…rewarding. Like a storybook fantasy."

"Are any of those places in our state?"

Storm huffed. "No. How about Tennessee?"

For Storm, that was probably as close as it was going to get. River wrote it down. "Close enough. What town?"

Storm rolled her ball and glove to the side, stood, and reached for River's hand. "Come on, let's find an atlas. I want to show you some places."

****

Even as Storm hauled River to her feet, she felt her conscious chide her. She had no business thinking of getting married. That was for River, and eventually Raine, not for her. She had a demanding job and serious obligations to attend to once River was married. Their

98

mother would accuse her of getting emotional like a silly schoolgirl, and wool gathering. No, she had no business wool gathering, or fantasizing, when she had significant weather-related matters to address. Important to the government. Rumored to be vital even to the health of the nation itself.

Chapter Seven

"Well, of course, she's hiding something," River commented, her voice pitched low. "It's the question of what."

"And how we can drag it out of her? She's so darn stubborn." Raine took a sip of her drink as she and River sat in Raine's backyard, taking in the sunshine, and staring at plovers and oystercatchers as they fished along the sound. A pair of colorful sailboats slowly chugged down the bay, heading for the open ocean. They were probably picnickers leaving the Currituck Light Station. The scent of jasmine and mint swirled in the breeze. Storm had promised to join them, and as they waited, they discussed the obvious fact she was hiding something from them. "But she won't lie. To her credit, she'll either avoid it or she'll tell us, but she won't lie."

Raine blew out her breath and studied her soda can. She turned it slowly so the sunlight bounced off the metal to create a rainbow of shiny colors. "It's the clever ways that she avoids telling us the truth drive me crazy. She's obstinate."

"Do you think she's in trouble?" River asked. "She said she had needed Brody's services, but what could he do as a property manager? She has no property except what's stuck to her shoe."

Raine grinned. It was true. Doubtful she'd ever

settle down and have a house of her own here in town. The expectation saddened her. She glanced at River and sighed. It would be something special to have both her sisters living here full time. She could regularly have them over for dinner and desserts. They wouldn't play games like they did when they were children, but there were other things they could do as grown sisters.

First, though, she and River had to figure out why Storm was so cagey since her return. She took a sip of her cola and let out a petite belch. "It's clear it's not his professional services she was after. Do you think he'll tell us what really happened between them?"

River chuckled at Raine's lack of manners. "If he won't tell us directly, I bet Calder could get it out of him. Those two are close. In fact, Calder probably knows what buttons to push to get the answers."

Raine smiled, and her face lit up. "Tell you what, I'll catch Brody alone, talk to him, and see if he'll just tell me what he knows. You talk to Calder and see if he knows any better ways to pull information from Brody, or better yet, offers to do it."

River extended her hand. "Deal. If Storm won't tell us what's going on by herself, we owe it to her to find out. It's for her own safety, after all." She lifted her soda can in a toast. "So, here is to Plan B, if we need it."

"If we need it," Raine echoed.

"What ya toasting?" Storm came up, slinging through the sand to join them. "Shaking hands and making toasts. What's up?"

"Sisters," River said.

"Weddings," Raine answered simultaneously.

Storm cast her gaze between the two of them,

101

finally reaching for the third chair and lowering herself. "So," she began slowly, "I fit in there somewhere."

River hastened to her feet. "Of course." She fished a drink out of the cooler and tossed it to her.

Storm carefully cracked it open, letting the fizz ooze off. She looked around. "Nice view here, kiddo. I dig the bamboo and the statues."

Raine smiled. "I find it peaceful. A place to unwind and tap into my creativity. I've so many plans for improvements." She flicked her wrist out. "I want to extend the bamboo walkway so that will wind along the sand to a meditation garden and fountain with koi pond over there. It will overlook the bay. And I can plant a few more shrubs like that Chinese maple over there."

"Sounds neat, sis. Real tranquil."

Raine shrugged. "A girl has to dream, right?"

"Here's to sisters and weddings and dreams." Storm raised her can into the air.

"Sisters and weddings and dreams," the other two echoed, lifting their drinks, as well. The clink of aluminum rang along the quiet shore.

"There is a store in Lady Beth, called The Silk Road, that specializes in Asian décor." Raine took a sip of her cola. "When we go for dresses, I hope to slip in a quick visit there, too, and check them out."

"That should not be a problem. We will have all day." River pulled her ever-present wedding planning notebook out from under her chair and flipped it open. "Now, about venues…Storm suggested a few places last night," she explained to Raine. "None of them near here. Actually, I've never heard of half these places."

Storm laughed. "They are all on US soil, sis, trust me."

Raine looked up. "Is that important, Storm?"

"No, why?"

Raine fiddled with the tab on her drink. "You could leave the country if you wanted to, right?"

"Of course I can." Storm started, her brows knitting together. "Much easier than either one of you could."

"Yeah, probably. And you can go anywhere on US soil you wanted to, right?"

Storm's eyes narrowed, and she slid a look between both sisters. "Of course, I can." She repeated the words slowly. "What is going on here?"

Raine shrugged "I'm just getting my facts straight as we figure out a location for River and Calder."

"Facts?" Storm wrinkled her nose. She set her drink aside and leveled a deep frown at her sisters, going to her feet. Her hands went to her hips, and she cocked one hip higher than the other, digging the other foot into the sand. "All right, you two. What's going on?"

Raine thought Storm looked like she smelled a rotten fish as she glared at them, her arms folded. She resembled Mom at the moment when she was waiting for a confession.

Raine and River exchanged looks. This reminded Raine of the time when all three of them went skinny dipping in the sound, west of town, and got caught by one of the boaters coming in. It was a rented pleasure boat, with a couple of cute boys on board. Storm, of course, rose out of the water like a mermaid, waving to them. River and she were mortified, all their fun vanished. And when they got home, and word was already waiting for them, and Daddy stood there like a lighthouse tower, glaring and waiting for confessions.

She considered sharing the memory and then decided it was better to stick to the present question of Storm's mysterious behavior.

River shrugged first, setting her own empty drink aside. She reached for Storm's arm. "We're worried about you. Are you okay?"

Storm laughed, a harsh, suspicious sound. "I'm fine."

"What's between you and Brody?"

She started to speak, then closed her mouth. She took a long moment to study the waves as they lapped ashore, and the birds fought over scraps… "It's too early to say," she finally said. "Though it could turn out interesting given enough time."

"What services did you need?" Raine pressed. "You didn't even know him."

"Ah-ha, the light has clicked. You think I'm in some trouble because I needed services from an unknown man, right?" Storm's eyes widened, and her tone flattened. She lifted her chin defiantly.

Raine stepped back from the stormy expression on her sister's face. Right then, her name fit. It wasn't anger; it was disappointment. She felt crushed under the weight of Storm's pained expression. She'd hurt her sister. She tried reaching out to Storm, but she pushed her arm away and stepped back.

"Well, rest assured, dear sisters. There is nothing serious between Brody and I just yet. And I am in no trouble. His services were something related to my work, and that is all there is to it." She handed her finished drink to Raine. "Now, I just recalled something I said I'd help Mom with, so I'll catch up with you later."

Raine started to call her back but stopped. She looked at River and shook her head. "That went terribly."

"On to Plan B." River nodded. She exhaled a breath that ruffled her bangs.

****

Brody absently stared at the waves and sunlight glinting off the water and boats tooting their horns and birds fighting over food. He breathed in the heavy sea salt air. The sunshine could almost be considered warm on his face, were it not for the unending breeze blowing inland. Yet he barely noticed any of it. He and Calder sat on the back of River's deck, beers in hand and thoughts on their minds. Brody's were more slanted toward a certain red-haired tempest.

"How would you feel about buying out my interest?" Calder asked.

Brody started, jerking, and his jaw dropped in surprise. Had he heard wrong? Surely. Thoughts of the bit of tattoo above Storm's creamy butt evaporated as he met his partner's somber stare. He muttered a curse, as the speculation of what her tattoo might be, and how much fun it would be to find out, slid from his mind. He blinked, mentally shifting gears and recovering from the most unexpected question he could ever imagine.

"Am I keeping you up?" Calder asked dryly. His lips pulled back into the tiniest ghost of a smile.

He latched onto the excuse, lest Calder tease him about dreaming of Storm. "Yeah, sorry, man, the dog kept me up most of the night."

"Really? Which one?"

"Uh, the white one?" he blurted out without

thinking. Darn, he knew he was busted as soon as his gaze landed on the white terrier lying contentedly at his partner's feet.

"Salt sleeps with me, and he never said a peep last night." Calder crossed his arms and leaned back in the chair. "So, what really kept you up? And don't blame the other dog, either."

Brody noticed Calder's poor attempt to hide his mirth as his cheek bulged as he stuffed his tongue in it to keep his smile at bay. He scowled and huffed in indignation. "I was trying to figure out what we're doing about our business. Our partnership. I called Matt last night for an update. Do you want to hear about how things are?"

Calder took a swig of his beer and exhaled. "I guess so. However, for the record, I think it was Storm Gallagher driving you to insomnia more so than worry about the firm."

Brody wondered where his sudden hostility was coming from. And how'd their pleasant break sitting on the deck with a couple of cans of beer turn so quickly. He shook his head. "At least one of us is worried about the business." He called Matt last night, without Calder beside him. "Our business, partner."

"Touché, Brody."

"So, what are you talking about buying you out? Why would I do that?" Fear, or panic perhaps, unknotted and unfurled like a flag in his gut. He set his drink aside, having lost all taste for it.

"Since I'm staying here in Sweetwater Harbor, I might have to consider selling my share of the firm. How would you like to buy it out?"

"Selling?" Brody echoed, feeling a sucker punch

hit to his gut. He jerked and felt his eyes round. Selling their shares had never, ever been part of any plan they'd talked about. Leaving Atlanta and ending their partnership had certainly not entered their minds, apparently until now.

"Don't look so panic-stricken, bro. It's just a thought. I'd give you a good rate below its fair market value, before going public." Calder shrugged and took a pull on his beer. "Then you could decide to either run it all solo with the staff you have or take on another partner. Maybe the next one might be a pain in the rear, though, so be careful."

"Like you're not?" Brody bit off, almost regretting it but not enough to cushion it with anything else. Calder knew him by now. That's why the suggestion of their partnership ending cut so much. He felt like his brother was saying he was leaving. "Let me think about it, okay? I wasn't expecting this out of nowhere, and I need time to think."

Calder grinned and nodded. "Yeah, I know how you are with surprises. I just wanted to let you in on what I'm thinking and give you time to consider an offer." He slapped Brody on the shoulder, then he sobered, his smile fading. "But really, man, I don't plan on going back there to live. I can't drag River away from here."

For one crazy, fleeting moment, Brody had to wonder which of the two fiancées were the lesser of two evils, River or Penelope. They both had inherited issues that were difficult to work around. River was just a whole lot more likeable. His challenge with her was just purely geographic.

"There you two are," River declared.

River's arrival broke into Brody's worried thoughts. He looked up and watched her slide the glass door open and step out onto the deck, followed by Raine and the black terrier.

"Do you need something, babe?" Calder asked.

Brody tried not to notice how his partner's face lit up like a holiday tree as she swept into his embrace. Nor how Brody caught himself automatically looking around for the third sister and the splash of disappointment that washed over him when he realized she was not there.

"Yes, actually I do." Raine looked at Brody. She beamed him a bright, hopeful smile. "Could you possibly come look at my car?" She jerked a thumb out toward the front of the house. "It's got this weird sound, and the mechanic is all the way in South Tides. I'm afraid to take it that far like this."

His experience with cars was limited to what sort of gasoline to put in the tank. But she looked so cute and hopeful, and she was Storm's sister. He slowly climbed from his chair. "Shouldn't Storm be looking at it? She seems to have the fundamental skills of a mechanic."

Raine shrugged, flicking her wrist. "She's gone off somewhere with Mom. Hard telling when they'll be back." She bit her lip. "If this is something serious—"

He held up his hand, halting her. "I'll look at it, but just don't expect a whole lot. But I'll try, okay?"

Beaming, she grabbed his arm as they entered the house alone. "Oh, thank you, Brody! I just knew I could count on you to try. I appreciate anything you can do."

He wordlessly followed her out to the driveway in front and waited.

She popped the hood on her small car.

He looked at the chrome motor. It looked like an engine. A shiny, clean engine. "So, what is it doing?" He rested his palms on the car's grill and wished again that Storm was there, for a few reasons.

"It's making a weird noise. Sort of like this." She screwed up her face and belted out a sound.

The noise reminded Brody of what a violin in the hands of a toddler might make. The kind of sound that sets one's teeth on edge. "Okay, that helps," he said, although it didn't. "Are you sure you don't want to wait for Storm to look at this?" He would feel better if she did.

"Well, she can, too, of course." She leaned her elbows on the edge of the car, still peering at him under her dark bangs. "You just met her on the way into town, right?"

He tried, and failed, to meet her gaze. "Yes." Memories too strong of their initial meeting swept over him. He hoped Raine would blame the heat in his cheeks with the bite from the wind.

"She needed you for something, right? Your help?"

"Yes." He moved hoses and wires around, but everything seemed secure.

"What it was about?"

What would make a beautiful woman take such a chance like she did? He'd been asking himself that for days now. He just knew it had to be important. "She's your sister, so don't you think you should be asking her these questions?" He didn't mean it unkindly; he just wasn't spilling any news she had not already told them. And bear her wrath. Images of a baseball bat sometimes would haunt his dreams of Storm.

Raine frowned, almost a pout. "I tried, Brody. But she clams up and changes the subject."

Yes, he'd witnessed that a time or two. He admired her skillful ease of switching and avoiding topics. Still…

Raine laid a hand on his arm and peered up through her dark lashes. "Brody, we're just worried about her. That's all. We just want to make sure she's not in trouble."

"We?" His eyebrows lifted.

"River and I."

Sisters to the rescue, no doubt. An emotion sliced through him, too rapid to identify, leaving a painful trail in its wake. He looked down at Raine's hand, gently gripping his arm, and back to her earnest expression. A weary sigh escaped. "Look, Raine, there is nothing I can tell you. I don't know the answers to what you're asking me. We met at the airport in Raleigh. That was our first encounter. We shared the flight in. That's all. Once we landed, we went our separate ways until we met up again here." He cupped her face in his palm. "Your sister is a very capable, strong woman. If she were in any sort of trouble, then I do believe she would come out on top." He cut her a grin. "And if she felt she needed to, she would share any concerns with you and the rest of her family. Since she has not, clearly, she is not unduly worried." If only he could believe his own words as easily as he said them.

She blinked, taking his words, and turning them over.

He watched as she sucked in her bottom lip and nibbled it, as he'd seen Storm do a couple of times. "You don't know Stormie though."

"No," he agreed. Though he was looking forward to their next meeting with renewed interest. "But I know her enough to think everything is okay."

By now, he knew better. Things were not okay with the fiery and lovely Storm.

****

"Oh, come on. Not you too, Calder!" Brody cried, exasperated as he glared at his partner. He dropped his hands onto his hips and immediately lost all interest in attending to his laundry. Why had Calder come hunting for him in the laundry room? Since when had Calder even been able to find a laundry room?

"What do you mean?" Calder placed his hands out, palms forward. "It was just a question. A harmless question."

Brody snorted, knowing better. What was it with these people? They were so nosy, constantly prying into every detail of a man's life. Honestly! He finished folding his clean laundry and placing it in a neat pile to put away. Calder had tracked him down like a deer at hunting season and was now starting on round three of the Spanish Inquisition, which he was getting tired of. And since when had Calder turned so nosy? Back home in Atlanta, Calder barely asked how his day was going, let alone question him on any personal stuff.

"Well, do you?" Calder persisted.

Brody ignored his watching him as he smoothed any possible creases from his pants before hanging them up. "Do I what? Wish to end this conversation? Yes, I do."

Calder moved to the wall and leaned against it.

Brody swallowed, nerves prickling along his arms. He knew that look. Still hoping for a defer, he bent to his task of folding shirts.

"You know, buddy, there is speculation among the Gallaghers that you and Storm have a history."

Brody's head shot up. "We don't. I barely know her." Though he planned on rectifying that shortly.

Calder lifted an eyebrow. "So, that's why she called you lover that day?"

He flushed, wondering what possessed her to say that. He ended with a shrug. "Storm. She's crazy. She probably says a lot of unexplainable and inaccurate things."

"So why are you caressing those chinos like that?"

His hand stilled over the fabric. What the heck was he doing? He shoved them on the rod and whirled to face his partner. "Okay, fine. So what is the speculation?" He watched Calder bite back a grin, and he wanted to punch him. Calder always loved to raise his ire, and if they really did part ways, he would miss Calder like he never missed anyone else in his life. Still, this whole inquisition thing was wearing thin. And he needed to speak to Storm to set some things straight. He reined in his impatience. "Well?"

Calder gave a shrug. "That Storm's in some trouble, and you know all about it."

Brody bit down on his tongue, choking back retorts. He ground his teeth and fisted his hands. Just wait until he saw Storm again. She would hear some ear blasting. He would get the facts from her once and for all, or he would spill the whole drinking fountain episode to her family. Let them tear that apart for a while.

He heaved a deep, shuddering breath, seeking patience. Calder would not get his goat. To rephrase

Cordell, he would not take scissors to his plans and patience. He absolutely would not push him into another slippery hole. "She put you up to this, didn't she? River?" Brody snarled as he glared into Calder's eyes. When Raine's sick car ruse didn't work to get the information they wanted, the sisters to the rescue decided to sic Calder on him. He read his answer in Calder's eyes.

He huffed a breath and grabbed another sweater, folding it rapidly. "Look, I don't know anything about her life. That is what I told Raine and is what you can tell River. Unless you want me to. I'll gladly confront your wife-to-be, if you're too scared to." He waited a moment to let the comment sink in before continuing. "I met her at the Raleigh airport. I know nothing more than you do. And"—his voice rose a notch—"we are not lovers."

"Fair enough." Calder moved his hands to his pockets. "But you'd like to be," he guessed out loud, jabbing back. "And I'll handle my own wife-to-be, thank you." Spinning, he headed for the door. "I'll tell her I talked to you like she asked, and you don't know anything. About anything." His dry comment hung in the air.

"Take a catcher's glove with you," Brody called in his wake, stepping over to the bench to sit. Suddenly, he felt exhausted. Was he too old to take a nap?

Chapter Eight

"Swallow your pride once in a while, girl," Muriel stated. "It's not fattening."

"What are you talking about, Mom?" Storm set the plastic tote down and turned to look at her mother. They were digging through storage totes in the attic above the garage, looking for things Muriel had stored away for the girls' weddings. She'd been an optimistic soul. The solemn stare sent a chill down her spine. She'd faced storms of epic proportions, hardly flinching, but that look from her mother made her want to run for cover.

Muriel planted both hands on her hips. "You know what I mean. We were wise as soon as you came back."

What made her so transparent around her family? She fiddled with a plastic tote lid and wondered if she should ignore her and get another tote or face her square.

"You are just being stubborn, girl," Muriel insisted.

She probably was, but her stubbornness was for their own good. The face-her-mother-head-on option finally won out. She blew out her breath and pushed the tote away with her toe. "Look, Mom, I appreciate your concern, but it's nothing serious. You can call off River and Raine now." She tried for a smile, not quite succeeding.

"If your sisters are asking you questions, it is only

because they are worried about you. As are your daddy and I upset. If you weren't so prideful, you'd accept a little interest in the vein it's intended. Eating your pride sometimes won't make you fat."

She blew out another breath, fiddled with her hair by twisting it into a thick braid, and thought for a moment. "Look, I can't really say anything except I know what I am doing. I have it under control. You guys just have to trust me."

Muriel sniffed. "If you don't know where you're going, you'll never recognize your destination when you arrive."

Storm considered that one. "Actually, my destination is pretty clear. I will be there once River is safely married." She planted one hand on her hip. "And why don't you bother Winter like this when he's around?"

Muriel smiled softly and patted her arm. "I do worry about Winter, just as much as I do you, but he has a whole group of people around him. You work alone so much."

She caught her mom's hand, gave her a reassuring squeeze, and then released her hold. "Not true, Mom. I have my team. We look out for each other, just like Winter's platoon does."

Muriel waved her hands, pursing her lips together.

Storm knew that look too. "Okay, Mom, I get it. You just need to know I am being careful, and my work is especially important."

"Is it dangerous?"

Storm hedged. That was sort of an abstract question. "No more than normal," she finally answered.

Mom's eyes rounded.

"But I feel the worth in the end is more than equal to any dangers," she hastened to add.

Muriel reached out, cupping Storm's cheeks. "I know what you do is always important, dear. And I trust you not to take any additional risks. But please be careful."

Storm wanted to say she always was careful, or she'd never take additional risks or something akin to that, but she could not give them voice. The look of worry in her mom's eyes pricked at her conscious as she pictured the two goons back at the airport. What would happen once she had to leave the safety of Sweetwater Harbor and reenter the real world?

"I will, Mom. I love you," she murmured, drawing her mom into a hug.

****

The desired totes were finally found and brought to the laundry room where Muriel promised to sort through them. Glad to have the project complete, Storm decided a walk along the beach was in order. She plopped on a ball cap and headed for the shore.

She liked to walk alone when she had things to think about. Out in the field, usually after a big chase, while her team was busy with their individual tasks, she frequently took off and walked. She simply strolled somewhere. Along train tracks, along rivers, along cornfields, along highways, wherever they happened to be, she just found a path, shoved her hands in her pockets, and placed one foot in front of the other. Eventually, she would return to her team and camp—when she was ready.

She slowly made her way across the dry sand. Oystercatchers, gulls, plovers, and sandpipers kept her company, wheeling and dipping overhead or scurrying across the sand and around clumps of sea grass. A few crabs shuffled out of her way. Altocumulus clouds laced the sky. The breeze blew in, carrying pungent scents of salt and mint. She inhaled deeply, not aware she had missed it so much. Even chasing hurricanes on the different coasts did not compare to this bit of North Carolina coast she knew as home. It was simply different, somehow.

Now, the way she saw it her mind was crowded with two main worries right now. First was the data she needed to get to her contacts, as soon as possible. Before another big storm came along that would take her away. Hopefully, the weather cooperated until River got married and she could sweep all those details up easily, complete with a pretty bow tied on top— metaphorically speaking. Automatically, she scanned the sky above, reading the signs it showed her. So far, so good—at least for here. But this was just one small corner of the world she chased.

And the other issue on her mind was Brody McGee. When time allowed, she liked to play around with the boys, just to see how far she could push them. Things felt different with Brody. First, he pushed back, which she found wholly interesting in and of itself. Seldom was the man who met her toe to toe. His anger was subtle and quiet. And—delightful to watch unfold. She could take a lot more of his kisses and still feel a need for more. She could dance in his arms and still wish for another song. She could spend time with him doing just about anything and find ways to enjoy it— and want more.

She watched a pair of sandpipers fight over a piece

of fish and decided Brody McGee was indeed wound up in her thoughts and life. She just didn't know how to get him out of it once she was ready to leave.

"Storm!" Her name ringing out snapped her head around. Instantly, something in her stomach took off in flight, like butterflies in a field. Her pulse quickened, and a smile swept over her lips. As if conjured from her thoughts, Brody McGee came striding across the sand toward her, his face a mask of emotions. She now realized she had walked from her parents' house along the shore toward River's house, from which it appeared Brody just came from.

Hands going to her pockets once more, she stood, waiting infatuated by the looks crossing over his face. Surprise first, a bit of anger and caution. Where could this lead? The journey—and the destination—was largely, up to him.

"I want to talk to you." He halted a foot away, hands resting lightly on his hips.

"Okay, about what?"

He stood, studying her. His gaze swept up to her ball cap, down to her bare toes, and settled on her face.

She would give a lot to know what he thought of her right in the moment. His hooded look gave nothing away beyond his first impression. Her pulse quickened as she waited for his answer.

"I want to know what is going on with you."

His bluntness made her eyes round in complete surprise. "I don't owe you any sort of explanation," she said, almost in defense. Now his expression could pass for impatient. What had gotten into him? "My life and business have absolutely nothing to do with you."

He laughed, a harsh sound, showing lots of teeth.

He reached out and snared her arm.

She moved close enough for her to smell River's brand of spiced coffee on his breath and feel the warmth on his fingertips.

"You came into town with secrets, and by God, you are going to share them with me. Right now."

She tugged against his iron grip, a bolt of concern rippling through her. "Let me go."

"Not until you start talking."

She fixed him with a dark glare of her own, lifting her eyes to his stony gaze. "You have no right to hold me against my will. You cannot demand answers. Now, unhand me this instant, you brute."

He laughed again, his voice holding a rough edge.

She tugged again, but there was no give in his grip.

"Since I've had the third degree from both your sisters, I think that entitles me to certain rights to hold and demand of you."

That brought a gasp of surprise. "My sisters? They questioned you?"

He nodded. "As did Calder, at River's request. They are concerned and thought I might hold some secret knowledge."

"Why would they think that?"

He pinned her with a sharp glance.

She flinched.

"Maybe the fact that our introduction in front of them began with you addressing me as *lover* led them to some mistaken conclusion," he suggested dryly. "Or the fact that you tried to drown me in the ocean during one of your many bouts of temper."

"I pushed you, not tried to drown you." She brought a fingernail up to her lips, nibbling thoughtfully. "You would have noticed the difference had it been an actual drowning attempt. And I am sorry for that."

He cocked an eyebrow. "Or perhaps it was you jumping a motorcycle over an open drawbridge after raising welts on my cheek," he added. "All good things to mislead someone. Now talk, Storm."

She blinked at his hard features, his teeth clenched in anger, and considered her options. He did not seem inclined to remove his iron-clad grip around her arm anytime soon. Her mom's words came to her and passed through quickly. What was it about staring at him that made them evaporate like rain after a thunderstorm on a hot day? He looked as though his thin thread of patience would not last much longer. Then what would happen? The thrill of the uncertainty spiked through her.

She gave a haughty laugh, and a slight toss of her head, letting the breeze catch her hair. "Do you think we're so different, Brody? We're both rainbow chasers, you know. The only difference is I know where to find my rainbows."

Brody blinked.

Astonishment flashed through his eyes, and she forced back a tart smile. She thought that might work to unsettle him. She waited for him to release her arm.

Instead, he leaned within inches, a hard snarl on his lips. "Woman, if you are trying to wear out my patience, you have a very long way to go." He backed up a fraction of the distance, his hard gaze pinning her.

That was not the reaction she was expecting or hoping for. Usually, if she stirred someone up enough, they backed away. Brody's grip stayed just as strong on her arm, indicating she did have a long way to go. So, how far would she have to push him? And what would she find once she got there?

Contemplating various choices, she finally surrendered with a heavy sigh. She glanced around to ensure they were alone, save for the ocean creatures. "Okay, fine. I have some weather data collected from my last few chases. The government is interested in it for development of search and recovery equipment and some other projects. It's all related to saving lives in buried rubble and predicting severe weather." She could almost picture her words working around his brain.

"Okay, what happened at the airport? Why did you need to accost me at the fountain?"

She hesitated. Would she be placing him in potential danger if she told him? What if the goons tracked her to town and discovered Brody? If might be better to downplay this.

He tugged her arm again. "If you don't tell me why you paid me, I'll tell your family about that passionate kiss."

Oh, that would be bad. Her family would totally overreact to his one-sided version, and River would probably make Calder be her bodyguard around the clock or something crazy like that. "Well, there are some folks who are trying to steal my information before I can deliver it to my government contacts."

"Why?"

His question came out hard and sharp. "To bury it? To keep it for themselves? Sell it to the highest bidder? I don't really know. I just know they are not the type to mess around with." She watched Brody's Adam's apple bob, and his face grew pale. His hold on her arm loosened enough where she could break away if she wanted to. Except she remained.

His eyes bugged out. "You are not willing to mess with them? Oh my God." He paused, his jaw dropping. "They were after you at the airport, weren't they?"

She silently nodded, almost feeling sorry for the guy.

"Keep talking."

A steely edge crept into his tone, and his gaze sharpened, sending a chill up her spine. What else did he want to know? "I'd picked up two of the henchmen somewhere. Probably on the flight in. I needed to give them the slip before I got on the next leg of the trip."

"So, what purpose did I fulfill?"

"A diversion."

He groaned, wincing.

She suspected whatever feelings and thoughts he'd had a few minutes ago just plummeted wickedly south. His Adam's apple bobbed rapidly.

"You are crazy," he said simply.

Though his expression promised it was sorely inadequate. Storm noticed his hand drop to his side, releasing her. She could get away now. Instead, she felt compelled to stay. Could she make him understand how important her work was? He'd commented before he did not understand her chasing but wanted to.

She laid a hand on his arm, watching his eyes spark. "My studies after disasters have already led to the invention of technology that helps search and rescue crews find people." She swallowed. "My work has saved lives, Brody."

"At the risk of your own."

She gave a slow nod. "Maybe. But I am skilled,

and my team is truly knowledgeable. We do not take unnecessary risks. But we do believe in the good of what we are doing."

"Which is?" His brows arched in twin peaks.

"Our findings and experiences in the field recently led to the creation of a device that can use microwaves to locate people. It depends on heartbeats and body temperature, instead of audible shouts for help. It works well alongside search dogs and cameras." She paused, her own heart beating faster with both excitement of her work and trepidation. Brody seemed to lean toward linear thinking. Could he possibly understand the importance of her work? "Can you imagine how beneficial that is not only in the wake of disasters like tornados and hurricanes, but to the government for bombings?"

He frowned.

She held her breath, trying to read his face and gauge his thoughts.

"Yes, I can see lots of far-reaching benefits for such scientific studies. In fact, at one level, it does excite me. But it also scares me too, when I consider how others would want that kind of information. How some unscrupulous people might stop at nothing to get it." He brushed a hand over her cheek. "Where is your information now?"

She hesitated, leaning back ever so slightly. "It's in a safe place."

"Storm."

His tone, clipped, carried no open threat. Just a promise of warning. She reached up, twisting the end of a pigtail around her finger.

He grabbed her hand, wrapping his fingers around

her slender wrist.

She remembered his iron grip, and an electric shiver spiraled over her.

"It's buried in a case behind Mom and Dad's house."

Brody smiled, his eyes taking on a faraway look. "Of course. Okay, if your henchmen show up in town, they will never find it buried in the sand. Like a pirate's treasure." He grinned. "I bet you buried it in the middle of the night, saying nothing to no one, so if anything is said or someone is questioned, they would have no guilty looks."

She nodded, surprised he thought like she had.

"And the way the sand blows around here, your diggings would almost immediately be covered over, erasing any signs of tampering."

Again, she bobbed her head. He was good.

He traced her jaw. "I admire the lengths you go to in order to protect your family."

"They're my family. I protect what's mine." His gaze was oddly tender, and his touch felt warm—both combined in sending a surprised shiver over her. But she felt he needed to be reminded of where her heart lay. "My family is my everything."

He grinned. "Yes, I recall your warning to that regard. I still think you're crazy. Like a fox." A wave of impulsiveness swept over his face, and he grabbed her by the waist. He hauled her into his arms. Next, before she could think, he dropped his lips to hers, capturing both her mouth and hand.

Heat ignited between them, and Storm pressed herself closer to Brody, her tongue exchanging barbs with his.

He grabbed a pigtail, working his fingers through the braided strand.

She moaned, a deep rumble, closing her eyes as she burrowed her fingers through his hair.

Pulling apart, he held her at arm's length, as he dragged in a ragged breath. "Woman," he growled, "I think I want another kiss. And I know you can do better."

She giggled and nibbled her bottom lip.

Capturing that lip in another deep kiss, he worked the buckles of her overalls loose as he pulled her down to the sandy shore.

Chapter Nine

Brody caught himself humming. He did not see the rich paneled walls of the Atlanta headquarters, nor did he hear the drone of voices around him. His mind was back on the shore with Storm. The table felt like sun-warmed sand beneath his fingers. He could not remember the last time he'd just spent time with a woman, kissing and hugging, giggling, and necking, and enjoyed it so thoroughly. Storm met him kiss for kiss and touch for touch. She was just as bold and wonderful as he'd imagined in his recent fantasies.

Seeing her start to nibble her index finger, he knew it was a nervous habit and barely resisted the urge to swat her fingers away. He could think of much better things to do with that mouth. He wondered how those lips might taste with another kiss. Then he'd quickly chastised himself. He needed to stick with his plan. Answers first—he needed answers from her. After that, well, after that he would see.

Once she'd thoroughly scared him with her truth about what happened at the airport and why she was on hyper-protective alert, he thought he'd scare her with some brutal kissing of his own. Folly! Without words, she informed him she was not to so easily intimidated.

And that suited him just fine. They'd made out, necking, kissing, and hugging like teens on the sandy shore. She'd confidently met every stab of his tongue and raked her nails along his neck and back. She had energy to burn, and he fantasized about testing her stamina.

If only he and Calder hadn't had to leave within the hour to return to Atlanta.

"Brody, man, you want to pay attention here?"

Calder's mocking tone reached over the conference table and slapped Brody back to the moment. He blinked, spread his hands over the laminate tabletop, and cleared his throat. "Yes, of course. You were saying?"

"Not me." Calder shook his head and pointed to his left. A telltale smirk promised he'd hear about this after their meeting with the staff of their firm. "Matt is trying to share important news."

Brody felt warmth spread over his face as he met Matt's puzzled expression. "Go ahead." He motioned toward Matt. "Continue, please." He reached for a water glass.

Matt began reading off his notes.

He ignored the amused look Calder shot him. Once their meeting with Matt and the key staff was complete, Brody disappeared to his office to assemble the hard copy files he needed to give Matt for disbursement. He had a few loose ends left to button up before leaving town again. He and Calder already went to their condos to pack and prepare before returning to Sweetwater Harbor indefinitely. Brody planned to keep his condo, but just shut it down for the time being, so he only needed to pack a few bags, including a set of formal wear, and lock the door. He didn't know what would happen during his next stay in Sweetwater Harbor, but he was determined to remain as Calder's wingman.

Calder was going a few steps farther by having furniture and personal items donated and hauled away. He did mention he was taking the last of his necktie collection back to Sweetwater Harbor.

Brody grinned. River was going to be so thrilled. Calder was also meeting with a real estate investor friend who was interested in buying the condo. All this extra stuff left Brody with more time to finish his tasks at work.

While he waited, he made phone calls to a few select clients, informing them Matt was their point person for the foreseeable future. They might not be happy with the news, but Matt was pleased with the hefty raise bestowed upon him today.

"Is Calder really moving back to that town? For good?" Matt came into the room and reached for the stack of files Brody handed over. "Sweetwater whatever?"

"Harbor." Brody nodded, a heavy sigh escaping him. "Looks like it. He's smitten with River and everything else there." Once they were married, he was losing a brother.

He checked the time. "He should be back from cleaning out his place anytime now." Once he arrived, and the rental cars were returned, they would drive their own vehicles the nine hours drive back to Sweetwater Harbor. Brody knew he had to return here at some point. But first, he had to make sure Storm and her family were safe and her precious data was delivered. He looked around the paneled walls, at their various certificates and awards, and shook his head. How had his life gotten so derailed? He'd gone there to bring Calder back, and now, he was returning to protect a wild spitfire gypsy.

Matt dropped the files on his desk. "Yeah, I find it hard to believe, too."

A mirthless smile crossed Brody's face. He stood and went to the full-length window. He was running out of fingers to count things that were hard to believe. He stared out the glass at the neighboring skyscrapers and shoved his hands deep into his trouser pockets. He felt at such a loss. How had his world spun out of control so quickly?

Were other people in those glass-fronted buildings staring out into the concrete, steel, and glass jungle and wondering where they took such a left turn in their lives? Or was he the only one?

Storm's taunting comment needled. Did he get out much? Of course. To the golf course. To dinner at one of the shiny windows below. To the movies or theater or museum. He seldom got out of town. Atlanta provided everything he needed or wanted.

And Storm? She was always "out there" in the middle of nowhere, and in small towns, and on the edges of big cities…anywhere the weather threatened. He shook his head. She was a hard person to figure out. She was a line stepper who couldn't wait to step over the line. She was a tumbleweed or a gypsy, just blowing from storm to storm and always chasing her next disaster hard. He'd never met a person more aptly named.

He sighed and leaned his head against the cool glass, wearily closing his eyes.

****

Storm stared out the car's back-seat window as their mom drove. She wasn't sure why River had to have shotgun, but their mom insisted because of her wedding that prompted this trip to Lady Beth, she needed the front seat, which left Storm stuck in the back with Raine. She felt twelve again and considered kicking River's seat.

"You know what this reminds me of, Mom?" At Muriel's murmur, she continued, "Those trips the five of us used to make to go shopping for school clothes. We'd ride in that ginormous SUV you had, that dark blue beast. I like this smaller one much better."

"I miss Big Blue," Raine countered. "I had much more room in that. Storm, you're hogging the seat!"

"Am not."

"Girls." Muriel's voice rang out. "Don't make me pull this car over."

Instantly, Storm and Raine stopped elbowing but shared a giggle and funny faces at each other.

River opened her planning book, cut her mom a wry grin, and flipped a few pages. Clearing her throat, she glanced back at Storm and Raine. "The mall has a bridal and formal store that seems promising. I already called ahead and made an appointment for two thirty. That will give us time to check out some other places too."

Storm peered over her sister's shoulder at the flowchart River had created. When it came to organization, River took top prize, with Raine coming in a close second. Storm never even started the race. She stared out the window as they reached the outskirts of town. For so long her experience had been to and from the airport and the quickest way in and out of town. She'd forgotten Lady Beth also hosted two shopping malls, restaurants, museums, galleries, and loads more.

Her mind flipped to Brody and their conversation late last night. They'd met on the beach, as the full moon danced on the water and waves gently lapped onto the shore. Brody traced his thumbs down her cheeks and along her jawbone. Then, he met her gaze.

"Let me come along when you go to Lady Beth," he had asked. "I can keep you safe."

She laughed, seeing first the hurt then the frustration cross his face. "Brody. You need to stay here. You would be so bored hanging out while we shop for dresses." She nudged him with her elbow. "I'm going to be so bored." She tried to laugh, to lighten up the mood and erase the seriousness on his face. "Stay here and do whatever bachelors did."

"I thought you knew everything a man should know."

He raked her a cocky grin that made goose bumps rise on her arms. "I only know the important things a man ought to know." She had tried to sound flippant, but deep down, she was really touched by his concern.

And now, in the light of a new day and stuck in the back of her mom's car with Raine beside her, she hoped she's made the right decision. If she were somehow tracked to Lady Beth, would she be able to protect her mother and sisters?

"Hey, do you remember girls' day out?" she spoke to no one in particular. "Dad and Winter would go out on the boat fishing for the day, and we'd come here for lunch, a movie, and whatever else looked like fun."

Her sisters joined in, sharing their favorite memories of various trips over the years. Who among them ever dreamed one day they'd make this trip to shop for wedding garb?

They reached the mall and roamed the stores until two thirty.

Mom found a bolt of aqua and tan fabric in the sewing store. She patted the cloth and smiled at River. "Look! Your exact colors. I can sew your ring pillows from this. And perhaps, something else small and new for you to carry."

"Isn't that the purpose of the bouquet?" Storm tried to hide her yawn, but she was already growing bored.

"It can be anything she wants it to be." Muriel tucked the bolt under her arm. "Let's go look at the ribbons."

Exhaling a sigh, Storm trailed after her mom and sisters. Sewing was another domestic duty she'd failed.

The group finally made their way to River's chosen bridal shop.

Storm studied the name above the pink and purple exterior. *Fairy Tales Bridal and Formal.* Hmm, she wondered about that. How many marriages ended in blissful fairy tales?

"Come on, you're slowing us down." Raine grabbed her arm and yanked her toward the doorway.

River checked them in.

Storm followed her mom and sisters, who followed the overly enthusiastic sales staff to a series of fitting rooms at the back of the store.

One lady removed the *Reserved* tag hanging on a blue velvet rope.

"Okay, each of you select a dressing room. We have Miss Gallagher's initial design choices on file. We will be in to gather measurements and bring the first round of wedding dresses, mother of the bride gowns, and bridesmaid dresses."

The first round? Storm exhaled heavily as she selected the last room at the end of the short hall. If they numbered the rounds like a boxing match, this could take a long time. She slumped in the chair and regarded herself in the full-length, three-panel angled mirror. Faded jeans, baseball jersey, ponytail, and scuffed sneakers. River had worn heels today, and Raine wore pretty, glittery ballet flats. Sometimes, Storm wondered if she really was related to them. How could they be so different?

She felt glad River was getting married, and truth be told, she was happy to be her best maid, or whatever her role was technically called. But, honestly, did she ever see herself coming to Fairy Tales one day and picking out her own wedding gown? Nope. That would be a big fat nope.

She sighed and rested her elbows on her knees and thought of Brody. Now, there was a man who could make her think of wedding bells and white dresses. Was he enjoying himself back in Atlanta? What if he decided not to come back? She brought her fist up to her mouth and nibbled a fingernail. She had no doubts Calder would return, but Brody was enough of a mystery yet to make her question him. She still doubted his true intentions when he first arrived in town. It didn't take a genius to see he had not come just to be at the wedding, so what was his real motive?

Excited gasps and sighs told her she wouldn't be alone much longer. The first round of dresses was arriving. What had River selected as her style? What would she pick as her colors and design if she ever wed? If she and Brody…

"Hi, I'm Amanda." One of the permanently perky assistants poked her head in the room and waved a length of yellow tape measure in the air. "Are you ready for measurements? The team is bringing the dresses."

"Sure." Storm stood and brushed herself off. "What do I do?"

Amanda smiled and motioned to the center of the room. "Just stand right there, arms out, breathe normally, and I will get all your important numbers."

As Amanda was zipping along with her yellow tape, another associate came in with endless yards of satiny turquoise and coral fabric.

"These colors are so pretty together," the new assistant gushed. "I just love them. They will look great against your complexion!"

Storm studied the colors and fabrics. Not bad. She could see why River selected them. What would she want as her colors? For a moment, while Amanda finished, she closed her eyes and tried picturing herself in a dress, walking up a church isle, to music…

Flowers and ribbons of emerald green, light plum, and glittery gold decorated the church in her mind's eye. Her bouquet was simple, draping with chrysanthemums, calla lilies, hydrangeas, and pansies, which matched the smaller bouquets on the ends of the pews. She reached the front of the church, and a man stood facing the preacher. She smiled at the sight of his broad shoulders, narrow hips, and cropped brown hair. He slowly turned, and her breath hitched.

"Miss Gallagher? Are you all right? Shall we start with this dress?"

****

Brody and Calder eased themselves into their Adirondack chairs, the wood still warm from the afternoon sun. To Brody's left, Cordell passed out the beer from the small cooler resting at his side.

"Well, boys, it won't be long till we're all related."

Brody's head jerked up at Cordell's comment. Related? Him? He mentally fumbled for the words jamming his mouth.

Then Cordell chuckled and wagged his beer can at him. A tiny bit of froth spilled out. "Relax, son. I meant Calder more so, of course, but seeing how you two are thick as thieves, it indirectly holds for you, too."

Brody unraveled that.

Cordell shot Calder a wink. "Unless there's something you want to share with us." He leaned close to Brody and motioned between Calder and himself.

"Umm, no," he stammered. His cheeks flared warm, and he ignored Calder's smirk. He swallowed the cold beer, wishing it could cool him down. The froth tickled his throat, but the drink did little to cool his embarrassment. He rubbed his palm on his pant leg and stared out at the blowing grass and sand. The stirring scene looked like the Sahara Desert out there. Where had Storm buried her data? All the bushes looked the same. How would she be able to find it?

As vital as it was, she doubtlessly had some way to mark the spot. Dimly, he heard Calder discuss his and River's next trip out of town with Cordell when he and River went to the pretrial hearing for Penelope tomorrow. He pondered that. River struck him as so in control of herself; he couldn't picture her coming unglued.

Cordell told a brief anecdote of a time when the

girls were younger, and River and Storm both came unglued over a prank Raine played. "Muriel and I thank our stars every night that all our kids have survived their childhood dramas and sagas and grown into responsible and happy adults."

Brody set his beer aside, the churning in his gut ruining the taste for more. "Aren't you worried about the risks Storm takes? Of her one day biting off too much?" His face warmed again under Cordell's unblinking stare, but he didn't care.

"I am a blessed man that all my children are happy, healthy, and courageous enough to chase their dreams. Remember this, dreams won't chase you, so you need to go out and chase them first."

Yeah, Brody got that. None of the women seemed to lack courage, especially Storm. However, he'd seen videos and pictures of some huge storms. Dangerous storms. He shook his head. "Yes, but don't you ever think she might run into something that's impossible to handle?"

"Son, Storm has never allowed the impossible to slow her down. None of my kids have."

Brody glanced over at Calder. He used to think he'd embraced his life with open arms, with boldness and bravery. But when he compared himself to Storm, he had to admit he was more of a coward than he'd like to think.

"Boys, do you every think that while you're out there living your lives, maybe your life is waiting? My little girls are good at living their lives to the very fullest. They don't look back at the end of the day and wonder what good their lives are doing." He paused and placed a palm over his heart. "They know. And I'm mighty proud of them." He picked up his drink and swallowed a slug.

Brody thought back to Storm's comment about whether he got out much. No doubt, she got out plenty and lived an action-packed, full life. Cordell's words echoed hers. Was he really living his life or making his life wait for him? A moment passed before his mind could wrap around such a strange concept.

He thought he had a good life in Atlanta. He had financial security, a healthy business, a nice place to live, a solid reputation, and he could get reservations anytime and anywhere he wanted. What else could he want?

He pictured Storm's zeal for living and absently fiddled with his can. She didn't make life wait. She grabbed it with both hands and held on tight, riding her life like it was a wild horse. And River and Raine did the same to a slightly tamer degree. No wonder Cordell was proud of his girls.

Finally, the old man placed his drink on the wood deck and raised his arm straight out toward the rolling waves.

Brody followed his aim.

"Boys, when a farmer plows a field, he keeps his eyes on the horizon. If he watched where the plow was, his rows would be crooked. Only by keeping his attention on what's up ahead can he stay straight." Cordell let his gaze travel slowly to Calder, and then settled on Brody for a moment. "And so it is with raising kids. Whether they be five or twenty-five. If I watched where they were right now, we'd be in trouble. I need to keep my attention on our horizon, then we'll be okay."

Brody didn't quite understand, but that seemed part and parcel for this place. Did that mean Cordell did worry about Storm's risks or that he didn't? He looked over at Calder and then shrugged.

Cordell sighed and set his drink aside. "Son, I can see you're a planner. You like to always have the ending in sight. My Storm flies by the seat of her pants. She has a hard time committing to dinner plans. She can be impulsive. That bothers you, but remember this—for lack of a shoe, the race was lost."

Brody had no earthly clue what that meant. He glanced at Calder, hoping for a hint.

Calder shrugged.

The move suggested his partner was just as lost. He exhaled and shook his head.

"Drink up, boys. The ladies will be back soon. We'll be expected to unload their purchases and listen to their shopping experiences." He slid his gaze over to Calder. "Best go on and get used to it, son."

To judge from the dopey grin on his partner's face, Brody had to guess Calder couldn't wait to do anything that involved time with River. A stab of jealousy knifed through him. When had he ever wanted to interact with a woman at that level? Never. Strangely though, he found himself eager to see Storm return. He wanted to help her unload her things and listen to her stories of their trip. It sounded…sublime.

If Calder could read his mind now, he'd tease him from now until eternity. He buried his newly discovered awareness behind another swallow of beer.

Chapter Ten

A horn tooted, and Cordell's weathered face broke into a big smile. He slapped his knees and leaned forward. "All right, boys, the ladies are here. Time to get to work." He pushed himself out of the chair and moved on toward the steps leading below. He paused and placed a warm hand on Brody's shoulder. He searched his eyes for a moment. "Son," he said finally, "you don't have to have it all worked out now. Tomorrow is always another day." He winked and descended the stairs with Calder.

Brody was left to turn it over in his mind. He heard excited giggles and slamming car doors echoing up the stairs. As he moved from the chair, he eased out a long breath. He was glad they made it back safely, but was he ready for sublime activities like Cordell described? Before he could steel himself for another round of Storm, there she was, her cute denim-clad derriere sticking out of the rear of the car as she picked up assorted bags.

"You girls all have a good time?" Cordell asked.

"I think we all had a wonderful time, dear."

Brody watched as husband and wife shared a sweet, brief kiss. A kiss that spoke of being happy to be together again. He sensed they didn't spend much time apart. He'd caught them holding hands a few times already. He pictured the kiss he shared with Storm at the airport, and his heart flipped over. Nothing was sweet about that. Hot…hard… He swallowed and listened to the happy banter of the group.

"We had a great time, Daddy!" Raine hugged her dad's neck exuberantly. "It's so nice to go away for the day. I'm glad I took a day off from the bakery. Even if I will have to work twice as hard to catch up now."

"You won't believe all the things we found for the wedding. It was utopia!" River exclaimed.

Cordell chucked. "I can see all the things, River. The whole back is filled to overflowing. You look like gypsies."

Brody watched as Cordell took the packages his wife extended and gave her a flirty wink before they headed up the steps.

River giggled as Calder reached around her slender waist to take her purchases, and she grabbed his wrists once he had his hands full. Calder playfully nibbled the back of River's arched neck.

He shook his head. Did those two ever stop with the public displays of affection? He'd never seen his partner so open about passion before. He approached Storm as she exited the back of the vehicle. Two pink bags bearing the name Fairy Tales in sparkly diamonds caught his eye. He could think of a few fairy tales of his own. He cleared his throat. "Can I carry anything for you?"

She whirled, her eyes narrowing.

Her benign expression changed to one of distrust. Now, how had he made her doubt him? Already?

"Nope. I got this, thanks." She stuffed one long box under her arm, looped a pink bag around her wrist, and hooked a third bag in her fingers. She pushed him out of her way as she moved toward the steps in her parents' wake.

The palm of her hand seared his chest as he watched her move away.

"Hey, Brody, I'd be ever so grateful if you could help me carry my stuff over to my car."

He blinked. Raine, the peacemaker of the trio. Whether she really needed the help or not, he appreciated her efforts. "Sure." He grinned. "What all do you have?"

She pointed out the same long box that both Storm coveted, and River had, which he had to assume concealed their dresses for the wedding. Raine had two small pink Fairy Tales bags, too. They probably all held much the same things, jewelry, and beauty accessories like shoes, or hosiery, or whatever. So, why did Storm have to push him away instead of letting him help carry her things? He shook his head, sure he'd never understand that crazy red-headed female.

"Wood? What does any of this have to do with the wedding?" He eyed the neat stacks of round wooden poles. He tapped a knuckle against the red dragon and Pagoda lantern statues. One was ceramic, and the other was resin. He shook his head again, this time more confused than before. This stuff seemed so out of place in the seaside town. He looked up at Raine.

She grinned and pushed a lock of dark hair out of her face. "Nothing. I bought these bamboo poles on sale and the other things to slowly work on my backyard oasis. The Silk Road store has the best selection for my style." She wrinkled her nose in a smile.

Brody melted. He'd move rocks uphill for Raine if she asked him to. Storm's little sister had a subtle charm that was completely different from her older sisters. He glanced back up the steps where Storm and her parents had disappeared and then reached for the first stack of bamboo bundles. "Are you going to build this backyard oasis all by yourself?" He followed Raine and transferred the stout logs into the backseat of her car. Not that he doubted she couldn't, if she wanted to. He was quickly learning not to underestimate the Gallagher women.

Raine settled the two statues on the floorboard. "No, River and Calder will help when they can."

Brody's eyebrows lifted. What would they do to help? Raine must have read his mystified expression.

"They build houses for the homeless. River's done it for years, and now, she's roped Calder into construction work, too."

Brody felt his brows furrow deeper. "Calder can swing a hammer?" Since when?

****

Storm turned the bike off and lowered the kickstand, officially parking the motorcycle back in its spot at her parents'. Her ride had not relieved much of her restlessness. She tilted her face to study the sky. The day was lovely, with lacy cirrus clouds hanging high in the sky. A mild breeze played with the ends of her hair and carried scents of salt and sand into the garage. She glanced around her parents' garage, knowing the hopeful tug in her chest had everything to do with the man on her mind. Ever since her mom, sisters, and she returned from Lady Beth yesterday, she'd been irritable and edgy. Finally, her mom suggested she take the bike out for some fresh air. Storm wasn't fooled and knew everyone wanted her out of their hair for a little while. And she was happy to oblige. Usually a few hours out on her bike settled her wanderlust and restlessness. Not this time. Less than a week remained before the wedding, and everyone's nerves were stretched taut. She just had her little secret adding to hers.

If only she knew what Brody's little secret was…

Then she'd know if he was—

"Storm! Mom wants you," Raine called, waving from the steps leading into the house.

"Dang, Raine. You almost gave me whiplash." Storm climbed off the bike. "What's the emergency?"

Raine moved aside as Storm reached the steps. She shrugged. "I don't know. We heard your arrival, and she just said for me to come get you." She moved off toward the driveway.

"Wait, doesn't she want you, too?"

Raine reached her car and opened the driver's door. "Nope. I need to get back to Sweet Obsessions. I am so far behind in orders; I don't think I'll ever catch up. I need to get some cakes and things mixed and into the oven. Bye." She waved merrily before closing the door.

Storm shook her head, dusted herself off, and jogged up the stairs. "Mom?" She found her mother in the kitchen peeling carrots. A pile of peeled potatoes rested beside a butcher-block cutting board and a long knife.

"Your dad caught some nice bluefish today, so fish chowder is on the menu tonight. Cut those spuds into small chunks."

Storm washed her hands and stood beside her mom, dutifully picked up the knife, and tested the edge. She blew out a breath and picked up a potato. Why couldn't Raine have done this before she left? She could have whipped this stuff up in her sleep. "Where is Daddy?"

"Napping. When you're done with those, go out to the patio and snip dill and basil, then chop them small. I also need a lemon zested."

Storm nodded, yet inwardly groaned. So much stuff to do for a bowl of soup! Couldn't they just go down to Bobbers and buy a few pints to go? This reinforced why she left the cooking to her mom and Raine.

Mom hummed for a moment as she scrubbed more carrots and long, skinny green onion-y things.

"There is something so calming, and satisfying, about cooking a meal from prep to eating it."

"I guess." For her mom and Raine maybe, but she hadn't discovered it yet.

"Just as there is a huge satisfaction in being a parent."

"I suppose so." She wasn't sure about that. The position seemed to have a lot of stress and sacrifices, too. She'd been no saint.

"To enjoy a lasting, loving relationship with someone special is a unique joy."

"Uh-huh." Storm slid the chopped potatoes into the tall granite stock pot where chunks of fish and golden corn already waited in a creamy broth. She breathed in the scent of raw fish and replaced the lid. Off to snip herbs.

"Which weighs more, Storm, five pounds of flour or five pounds of cotton?"

Storm riffled through the top drawer for the designated herb-cutting shears, paused, and looked up sharply. "The flour, of course."

Muriel stared, steady, unblinking, her head tilted slightly. Her palms rested flat on the counter as she waited.

Storm squirmed, thinking the question through.

Finally, Mom raised an eyebrow.

The barest twitch of her lips made Storm want to smack herself. "Oh, duh. Neither one. That was a trick question, Mom. No fair."

Muriel smiled and reached to pat her cheek. "Storm, my dear wild one, the world is just full of trick questions."

That was a true enough comment.

"Before this day is done, Storm, I want you to go find Brody and apologize."

Storm quivered at the stern look in her mom's eyes. She knew that look but hedged. Apologize for what? Heaven knew she had a long list.

"How about we just round it up to general rudeness? I'll bet you still haven't apologized for pushing him into the ocean or slapping his face. Add the sharp way you spoke to him earlier when he just offered to carry your things from the car."

"But, Mom—"

Muriel held her hand out. "But nothing. There is no good reason to be curt with someone who is only offering to help. I raised you better. Remember, you can't pour something out without getting a little on yourself." Muriel patted her arm. "And this time, make sure your apology is genuine. Now, go snip herbs."

Storm watched her mom walk away, and she opened and closed the scissors she held. At least, her mom had not said anything about someone coming along with scissors every time she thought she held the world by a string, like her dad was likely to say.

****

"Bro! Man, I can't stand seeing you like that."

Brody's head shot up. He blinked, needing a moment to reorient himself. He looked around at River's living room, the laughter coming from the movie on the television, and lastly where Calder and River sat cuddled on the sofa. He bit back the automatic sigh that Calder's arm would naturally be wrapped around River's shoulders and neck like an anaconda. Her contented smile both warmed his heart and chilled him all over. The three of them sat ringed around the television, watching some documentary.

And his thoughts wandered in countless directions. Calder. The firm. The lives they put on hold in Atlanta. Storm. His brain stalled there, like the eye of the hurricane. He sucked in a deep breath. "Like how?" As if he didn't already know.

"Bro."

Calder's expression said it all. He'd been a million miles away, again.

River shifted her hair around, letting it fall to drape over her other shoulder. "Bro? Is that short for Brody or Brother?"

Brody and Calder looked at one another, both their eyes widening. Brody took that as clear evidence neither one ever really thought about it. Calder just started calling him that about a year or so ago. He'd never questioned it. He shrugged. "Either one, or both." He looked back at Calder, who also raised his shoulder.

"Men." River moaned and shook her head. "You do look a little spacey, Brody. Everything okay?"

"Fine. Just thinking about things."

River nodded and returned her attention to the show now that the commercials were done.

Calder continued to stare.

The look pressured Brody to think of something to offer as his tangled thoughts. He grabbed one from the mess in his mind. "Explain this to me; we are both successful men in our thirties, and we are well respected in our field and by our colleagues. Why is it here, we are reduced to 'boy' or 'son'?"

Calder laughed. "That's what you've been thinking about?" He removed his arm from River's shoulder and captured her hand.

"Yeah." True enough. It had crossed his mind a couple of times.

"That's just the way it is here. There are loads of local expressions and habits indigenous to the area. It's part of the timelessness." He shot River a sweet smile. "Since most people remember me at least from when I was young, I'll always be a boy or son in their eyes. I guess you're included by association."

"Great."

Again, Calder chuckled. "Look, it's a nice evening out there. Why don't you go for a walk?" he suggested. "Walk the shore, walk the road, or walk the town. Clear your head, buddy. Get some fresh air. Maybe the fresh paint fumes are clogging those infamous planning brain cells of yours."

Despite Calder's light, teasing tone, Brody still picked up the thread of concern coming from his friend. He glanced outside. The sun was sinking, not quite to the horizon. Streaks of purple and pink danced across the water. It would be a pleasant night, and he did feel cooped up. "You're right. I need some fresh air." He got to his feet and stretched, rotating his waist from side to side. "I'll see you two in a little while."

"We'll leave the front door unlocked," Calder said.

Brody reached the door. He laughed. As far as he'd learned, everyone left their door unlocked in this town. He still had a hard time wrapping his head around that. No one appeared to lock their vehicles, either. It made him believe the locals put a lot of strength on honesty.

He descended the stairs, dropped his hands into the pockets of his jeans, and struck out for the beach. He soon picked up a trail of *U*-shaped prints in the sand and followed them along the shore.

He was a space case lately, and he knew who was responsible for turning him into one. Images of an unforgettable red-haired firestorm flashed through his mind like wildfire. Her laughter tickled his imagination, and her sweet perfume teased his nose. He could not get that woman out of his mind!

What was he supposed to do?

He knew what he wanted to do, but what should he do?

****

Storm sat on the sand, just out of the tide's incoming reach. After spending almost an hour preparing vegetables and herbs for dinner, she eagerly escaped as soon as she could. She picked off pieces of a slice of bread she'd nabbed on her way outside and flicked them out into the water. Plovers, seagulls, and oystercatchers raced through the shallows to snatch up each piece. The birds' screams and squabbles matched her mood. The ocean breeze tickled her face. She breathed in the cool air spiced with salt. As much as she loved traveling, she also loved being back here. Except, her mom was getting exasperated with her lately. Darn her protective instincts. Darn that Brody McGee for stirring them up.

For her mom to be exasperated with her or Winter—or both of them—was nothing new. She wasn't proud at how much she could aggravate her mother just in the way Brody made her feel and react. She tossed out a couple more pieces of bread, and the birds swooped in.

What was it about Brody that raised all her defending tendencies? She suddenly felt fifteen again. She'd only meant to keep him from peeking at her pretty bridesmaid dress and the sweet little black number she's added to her purchases. And somehow, when he innocently offered to carry her things, she'd morphed into a mama lion that should have made her own mom proud.

Instead, her mom read her the riot act about being so mean to Brody. Why did he push her buttons? Lots of her buttons? She sighed, flicked out the last of the bread slices, and closed her eyes, pushing the sounds of fighting seabirds from her mind.

Whistling reached her, and she opened one eye, looking for the source.

Brody came strolling along the beach, hands in his pockets, his head bent, and the same short tune playing on his lips.

She smiled, remembering those lips. Maybe he irked her so easily because she liked him? But could she trust him? "Hey, lover."

He frowned. "I don't think that's an appropriate name."

149

She smiled, then shrugged, not really caring if it was appropriate or not. It annoyed him like he irritated her. Good enough.

He stopped about ten feet away. "What are you doing?"

"Sitting here, feeding the birds." She paused. "Thinking about you."

His face brightened, and his frown slipped a little. He looked her up and down, tilting his head to one side. "What about me?"

Kissing him again? Nah, better not say that. She climbed to her feet and brushed off her back side. "I need to apologize, um, for pushing you in the water, for slapping your face, and for snapping earlier today down at the car."

He cocked a crooked grin. "That's quite a list, Storm. Did your mom put you up to that?"

Sometimes, like now, his perception startled her. She nodded. "Can I tell her I apologized, and you accepted?" She watched as he turned the question over, her chest suddenly heaving.

"Sure. I think we have bigger things to think about than your occasional temper tantrums." He closed the distance between them.

She smelled cool mint on his breath, so he must have either just brushed his teeth or chewed some minty gum. He looked deep into her eyes, making her breath catch. Any thought of taking offense to his temper tantrum comment faded with the salt winds.

"Calder and River leave tomorrow for that court thing with Penelope. The wedding is in four days. When do you think you can safely take your data to its destination?"

That wasn't what she thought he might want to discuss. "I'm not sure. I'm not in too big of a hurry. I want the airports to clear out first. If there are any more random goons flying around, scoping out the hubs, I want them to get tired of coming up dry and just give up. So maybe next week. Why?"

He reached out and took her right hand into his. "I'd like to go when you do take it."

That's twice he surprised her. "Mumm, that's okay. I can get it there."

He smiled. "I never said you couldn't. I said I wanted to accompany you. Two can protect it better than just one." He paused, another crooked smile flashing over his face. "Besides, if you need another distraction, I want to make sure I'm handy."

She grinned at his cheekiness. She moved a strand of hair behind her ear and tilted her head to one side. "We could just jump to the distraction part right now…consider it practice."

"Storm, believe me, I don't need practice," Brody purred, his voice a deep rumble.

His rough growl sent shock waves over Storm. His fingers capturing her chin and his warm lips touching hers convinced her.

Chapter Eleven

Brody had never met someone better named than Storm Diana. Her electric touch and her demanding kiss were powerful, engulfing him like any weather-related storm. They left him reeling and disoriented. He closed his eyes and felt the strength and determination of a woman who took what she wanted from life. And from him.

Finally, regretfully, he pulled back from the kiss and drew in a ragged breath. He looked at her from lowered lids. "Woman, you should come with a warning label," he rasped. The way his chest was pounding, an uneven breath was the best he could manage.

Storm giggled, her eyes lighting to match the sinking sun behind them. "You complain too much, Brody." She grabbed his hand and tugged him through the sand. "Come on. I have an idea."

He lifted an eyebrow at her words. Any idea from her was bound to be something else and nothing short of crazy. As he followed, he eyed the towering posts of her parents' home and then balked as they reached the stairs. "I'm really not in the mood to visit right now." He was selfish and wanted to keep Storm to himself.

She chuckled again and yanked harder on his hand, nonplussed at his reluctance. "Me neither, silly. Trust me."

Trust her? His heart thumped. His mouth dried. His every instinct said that could only lead to trouble, but he surrendered anyway and moved to match her pace. He'd seen or been a part of enough trouble since meeting Storm than he'd ever experienced or witnessed in his life before. He felt confident he could handle whatever she had in mind this time. He swallowed hard. "I'm trusting you, woman."

She laughed and led him past the stairs, under the house stilts, and out to the parking area. He still felt uneasy being under the house. He looked up at the bottom supports, and he realized that was all that kept the lofty structures standing. Call him cautious, but he lacked the familiar ease everyone else had when going under a house held by poles in the sand.

Fleetingly, he wondered if this family would enjoy one of those crazy roller coaster rides that raced toward a lake or cliff before savagely catapulting riders off into another direction mere breath-stealing seconds from launching off the track into space. As for him…that's a solid nope.

How did Calder satisfy his yen for adventure all these years? Coming from this place, he must possess the same sense for thrills or danger. Why had he never noticed any fearless tendencies in his partner? Maybe he quietly fed it while driving the interstates that twisted around Atlanta.

They reached her multipurpose vehicle, not quite a typical SUV but not a standard four-wheel drive wagon either. It was a sporty, high-wheeled middle child.

Storm placed one hand on the top and opened the driver's door, looking across the roof at him. "Come on, Brody, get in. You're not scared of a little fun, are you?"

Her teasing smile stirred up all sorts of ideas in his mind. *Fun? With her?* "Of course not." He climbed in. The interior was clean, though full of music CDs, hair ties, haphazardly folded maps stacked in a pile, and a half-empty—or half-full—cup of leftover soda. Her red lip gloss left a faint red ring around the extended straw. He settled into the bucket seat and glanced over his shoulder. The small bench seat behind led to a short cargo bed and ended with a drop-down tailgate.

She started the engine and shot him another heart-stopping smile. "Okay, here we go," she purred as her hand dropped to the shifter knob. She drove out to the paved road and headed north out of town.

The ocean stayed on Brody's right, and he split his attention between the lapping waves and Storm's red tresses flying out the window. The paved road gave way to sand. She edged closer to the ocean to avoid the sand dunes that crept toward the Atlantic. Sea birds lifted into the air or scurried out of their way.

"Only four-by-fours can drive through here," Storm explained.

Brody could see why. "It seems isolated. No more houses. No more trees." Looking around, Brody just saw endless sand and water…stretching out for miles…like they reached the end of the world.

"Not so isolated. Virginia state line is just up there a short distance." She parked and turned off the engine. "It's almost dark. We'd better hurry."

Adrenaline pumped through Brody as he followed her lead and exited the vehicle. He had no clue what she had in mind as fun. They were alone at the world's end, and it was getting dark. He watched as she crawled into the back of the cargo bed and dragged a plastic tote to the dropped tailgate.

She took the lid off and motioned to him. "Come help me carry this over there."

Dutifully, he complied, eyeing the driftwood and bent limbs inside with confusion. He silently noted how she made it an order and not a request. He carried the tote himself, brushing her aside. "I have this. Now, where to?"

She led the way to a sandy spot about twenty feet away, and she reached for the wood before he even had the tote set down. She stacked the timber and then struck a match. The dry firewood instantly shot orange and red flames into the gathering night. "Next, a little mood music." Storm returned to the truck and flipped on the radio.

Soft strands of piano, violins, guitars, and the steady beat of drums filled the air. Crickets chirped the melody. Lapping waves added harmony. Shivers ran over Brody. This was altogether, something…completely unplanned for him…and clearly planned by her. No. He reconsidered. She didn't plan this. She was just embracing life and seizing the moment as it came. Her youthful impulsivity and nature's whimsy were conspiring against him now. Another shiver of electricity rolled over him like ocean waves. He coughed, clearing his throat. "Storm…"

"Shh. Just listen, Brody." She moved to the tailgate, backing up to it. "Lift me up."

Again, an order…not a request. He sighed. He placed both hands on her hips, breathing in her unique scent. He kept his eyes fixed on the tiny braid near her ear as he lifted her to the tailgate. He steeled himself against the paradox of her muscular strength and womanly softness.

Once he deposited her safely on the tailgate, he backed away as she stood. The cool tickle of misty air brushed against his cheek. The brisk bite of salty brine swirled around him. He stepped over U-shaped imprints in the sand. He was so intent on watching Storm, he barely noticed any of them.

She caught the groove of the music and closed her eyes, lifting her arms and swaying to the slow beat. The moon shone on her shoulders, bare where her shirt slipped low, and teased her red-blonde locks.

He stood there, hands hanging at his sides, his chest tight as he forgot to breathe as he watched her sway. Something uncoiled inside him. He tried to drag his gaze off her—to the water, to the sand, to the moon, anywhere. That was as impossible as lifting an eighteen-wheeler truck by hand. He surrendered, with a sigh, and watched her dance with the rising moon as her backdrop. She was…in a word…captivating.

She reached up, tugged her ponytail holder loose, and tossed the elastic circle to the ground.

Brody bent and retrieved it, slipping it in his chinos with the intention to return it after her dance. He alternated between watching, his heart rate accelerating and then stalling when she changed moves. He could not have spoken if he wanted to. She might have to give him mouth-to-mouth yet. He tried to swallow, but his throat convulsed at the thoughts popping in his mind.

Suddenly the music stopped, and she stood still for a moment, blinking.

"Storm? Are you all right?"

"Yes." She extended her hand, wiggling her

fingers. "Come up here. There's something I want you to see."

Whatever had uncoiled within him before now snapped like a spring. His mouth went dry. His hair stood on end. His gaze shifted from her to the tailgate.

"Brody."

Her tone held no question; it was all directive. Okay. He leaped up and joined her.

She spread out a thick blanket and lowered herself to it. She patted the spot next to her.

Brody obliged. She settled against him, resting her head in the curve of his shoulder. Her wavy hair tickled his nose. Mild florals and fruity scents of apple mixed with cinnamon mixed with the wild sea salt. He tucked his arm under his head to use as a makeshift pillow.

"Have you ever stared into the sky, Brody?"

"I don't believe I have."

She raised her arm to point upward. "That's Orion's Belt, part of the Orion constellation. Follow the stars to the Big Dipper. There is Jupiter. It looks like a star, but it's really a faraway planet. And those wispy clouds are called…" She droned on, talking about clouds, stars, and all things sky and weather.

He soon gave up trying to understand. He waited for her to take a break. "Tell me, how did you get into storm chasing?"

She shrugged, her shoulder pushing into his chest. "It started out as something fun to do between semesters while I was studying astronomy. It didn't take too long before I was completely hooked. I wanted to take my newfound passion and do something big with it."

As if this woman could bother doing anything

small or insignificant. He chuckled. "I'd consider just chasing storms as something big." He had to admit he was impressed with her studying astronomy. Beneath her wild heart, she had intellect.

She was quiet.

He wondered what she was thinking.

"Even the term storm chasing sounded cool."

He felt her smile behind the words and had to grin himself. "And?"

"And I quickly saw the bigger picture of chasing, the hard work and dedication chasers gave, and the many ways it would help humanity. I finished that summer, went back, and switched my majors to atmospheric science and meteorology."

"Double majors? You're a smart cookie." He was fully astonished now. He gently tapped a finger alongside her skull and marveled at the softness of her hair as he lingered in her tresses.

"What? You thought I was just a ditzy groupie who followed the chasers like a happy little cheerleader? There is a lot of science, planning, and safety that goes into these chases."

Brody turned his head to one side, studying her. "You'd look great in a cheer uniform."

She giggled. "I might not be the salt of the earth like my sisters, but I do have a good brain." She sighed. "They are so practical that paying a bill on the due date is living dangerously for them. But they show their intelligence every day. I'm the opposite. Winter, too."

"Umm, I think you have a lot more than just a good brain, Storm." He now trailed his fingers down her jawline and then moved to her collarbone.

She closed her eyes.

He had never felt so right in his life. This…them being alone on a beach, fire burning, lying in a truck bed, and watching the moon kiss her skin while waves washed ashore. It was all blended together to make him feel so perfect. He could ask for nothing more.

This was a moment he'd happily die for. He had to keep the feelings going, keep her talking, and keep her lying next to him. "No more teaching me about clouds and weather? I found it fascinating." He paused, thinking of his words. "I find you fascinating. But first, tell me about those tracks I keep seeing on the beach." He traced a *U* on her arm.

"The wild horses who live around here. There are a couple of herds who have lived here for generations and pretty much make this area their own. They eat in people's yards, right up to the front door sometimes. I'm surprised you never noticed them before."

He shrugged. "Guess I've only had eyes for you, not wild horses."

Storm's free hand curled up and entwined with Brody's hand. "It's not enough to say it's cloudy on a given day. It's more important to say what kind of clouds are involved. Most clouds can be classified as happy or as angry. Happy clouds examples are the cirrus and cumulus. They sail in the higher air currents. Angry clouds could be the stratus and cumulonimbus. They travel in tighter bunches and tend to be lower to the ground."

"Let me guess. They bring the rain?"

"Yes. You earned a kiss." She twisted around, hoisted herself on one elbow, and looked down into his eyes. She dropped one palm on his chest, then lowered herself to his lips.

He lifted his head to meet her, capturing her lips in a salt-tinged kiss. They parted, and he watched her lick her lips. He already wanted another wet kiss. He licked his lips, tasting strawberry-flavored lip gloss. Her smile was coy, and her eyes bright. "So, how would you feel about staying out here, under the stars, and kissing all night long?"

Her words almost stopped his heart. He drew in a breath, chuckled, and scenes painted themselves in his mind. He would need mouth-to-mouth for sure. But a person only lived once, and he supposed living around Storm was as delightful as it was dangerous. He hooked an arm around her neck, bringing her close. "You just read my mind."

Chapter Twelve

"I know a secret," Raine singsonged as she waltzed into the laundry room.

Storm looked up from her task of folding sheets. "You do, huh?" She tossed half the fitted sheet toward Raine. "Tell me all about it after we fold these dumb things." She inclined her head toward the basket brimming with sheets, towels, and assorted linens.

Raine picked up the corners and spread them to arm's length. "Mom in a cleaning frenzy again?"

"I guess. Something about having things ready for the wedding. She said Daddy and I were going on blow-up mattress detail later today. What that has to do with sheets and towels and stuff is beyond me."

"Everyone's coming—aunts, uncles, and most of our cousins. Mom's mission is hospitality and where to put everyone. Winter will stay here. Maybe a couple of others. River's house is close to full. I'm hosting a few. Hotel can only hold so many. Maybe the Finn house will get drawn into this."

Storm nodded. "That's what River and Calder said when they discussed it with Mama and Daddy before they left town."

Raine shook her head. "I bet that pleased Calder to no end. He told me once he wished the whole thing would collapse and get dragged into the ocean."

"That does happen. Maybe he'll get his wish."

Together they folded the fitted sheet. Raine brought her ends to Storm's and tucked it into a neat square. "Hand me another one." She beckoned Storm.

"What is the point in this?" Storm lamented. "We just go and wash and fold them all again afterward."

Raine shot her a wide-eyed look, and her jaw slacked, followed by a shake of her head. "Oh my word," she murmured incredulously.

The sisters folded the sheets and blankets. Finished, Storm exhaled. "Thanks, little sister. The rest of this stuff won't be so bad now. Okay, what's your secret?"

Raine's grin almost split her face. "You didn't come home last night."

Storm felt her cheeks flame. Her parents possibly already knew if Raine also knew. Well, not the first time she'd done something like this, but now she was an adult. She met Raine's amused smile. "So?" She folded a towel, carefully plucked a couple of pieces of lint, and smoothed out any wrinkles.

"I bet I know where you were."

"I bet you don't know half of what you think you do."

Raine just grinned at Storm's retort. "Maybe." She lifted her shoulder in a shrug. "Or maybe not. In this case, I think you were out with Brody. All. Night. Long." She started snapping her fingers, dipping her shoulders, and singing the hit 1983 Lionel Ritchie song. "All night long…"

Storm groaned loudly and shoved Raine. "Okay, I get it. Please don't sing. Don't try to sing. You can't."

"Ha." Raine plopped on a step stool and rested her elbows on her knees. "What's he like? Really? He seems nice."

Storm nodded, still folding creases from the towels and washcloths. Memories of lying in the back of the truck, stargazing, talking about all sorts of stuff, and mercy, the kissing filtered through her mind. He was nice. And sexy. And a great kisser. And a lot more. "He is a kind man." She shot her sister a wicked smile. "I'm just not sure what kind of man he is."

"Oh!" Raine snatched a hand towel from the pile and snapped Storm's hip.

Storm grabbed a washcloth and flung it at Raine. The damp cloth splatted against Raine's arm as she tried to catch it and fumbled it like a football.

"Stormie!" Raine screeched playfully.

The moment felt so right to Storm. She'd missed this craziness with her sisters.

They giggled and tossed pillowcases and towels at one another, trading good-natured insults.

"Girls! Tell me that isn't clean laundry you're both tossing around." Muriel's voice rang out.

Storm and Raine stopped, sobering as they studied the piles of washing scattered on the floor. They both bent to retrieve it, carefully folding.

"Umm, yes, they were clean," Storm confessed.

"And now they're not." Muriel shook her head. "You two. Storm, go find your father and start blowing up mattresses. Raine, stay and help me here. We also need to work on the menus."

"Yes, ma'am," both sisters murmured and moved to follow instructions.

Just before she crossed the laundry room doorway, Storm reached back and pinched Raine on the arm. "All night long," she whispered as she fled the scene.

****

Brody was glad Calder and River were gone. He wanted some time alone to process what happened last night. He stood on the deck, watching the two terriers running through the sand and barking at one another. As their houseguest, he'd offered to care for the dogs while they were out of town. While he hadn't owned a dog in more years than he could remember, he did like them. And the terriers were a winsome duo.

They came racing back finally, panting excitedly.

He let them inside and gave them each a bone treat from the special jar on the counter.

They took their snacks to their beds and lay down after circling twice in opposite directions.

One white and one black, the perfect ying and yang for his twisted life. As crunching sounds filled the air, he had to chuckle. Someday, he might consider getting a dog when his life became stable. Right now, he worked too many hours at the firm to adequately care for a pet.

He smiled at the scruffy pair and then filled his coffee cup, added a splash of cream, and carried it to the sofa. He picked up the journal and pen he always carried. It held thoughts, observations, poems, and more from over the years. Not even Calder knew he kept a journal. He flipped it to the next blank page, adjusted his grip on the pen, and leaned back into a comfortable position.

After last night, out on the beach with Storm, he needed quiet time for serious emotional processing. He'd never felt so right, so alive, in all his life. He wasn't sure what he'd been holding inside, but as he'd watched her, and caught little peeks of her mysterious tattoo, he suddenly felt himself lose it.

If he recalled correctly, Jane Austin once said, "To be fond of dancing was a certain step toward falling in love." He smirked. Who said guys couldn't be romantic? And watching Storm dance was certainly a step toward his heart falling for her.

The nagging worries about the firm faded away on the beach last night. Now he understood how Calder could so easily say he wanted to remain in Sweetwater Harbor. Brody was having a hard time picturing himself driving away for good.

And now he had to figure out what to do after Calder's wedding and Storm's data was delivered. He knew he was absolutely going with her to deliver it, regardless of how much she might balk. He wasn't itching to meet up with guys she was unwilling to deal with, but he'd be damned if he let her face the chance alone.

He fingered the elastic hair tie on his wrist. He'd forgotten to give it back. For now, it was his souvenir. He lifted it to his nose and inhaled. It still held the strawberry scent of her shampoo. He'd not come to Sweetwater Harbor to fall in love. His life would be just fine if he could only have taken Calder back. But after last night, he knew he had to seriously rethink his plan. The wild and beautiful—and double major intelligent—Storm Diana has shifted his thinking. He put the pen to paper and began writing…

I wasn't looking for anything, I was good, until you took my breath away.

I thought my life was fine, then my heart skipped, and my thoughts ran away.

Out of the storm, one look into your eyes, you took

aim and shot a dart.

It's mild to say you were a surprise, and your aim was true straight to my heart.

Now I'm left to ask myself, what should I do? How can I choose?

I'm caught in your gale; you took my plans and left me confused.

Wild Tempest, you grabbed my attention and then my heart and mind.

Last night, just the two of us alone, I felt your soul whispering to mine.

Now I'm caught in your gale. Hurricane, you

Brody's hand trailed off, the pen slipping off the notebook's page. The poem wasn't bad, but it needed work. For now, it was a start. The thoughts of his heart. He lifted his gaze from the words on the page to the hair tie on his wrist to the sparkling waters of the bay outside of the window. He tracked the path of a red-and-blue sailboat, its huge white sail snapping in the wind. Hurricane. He laughed mirthlessly. Yes, he sure was caught. So now what?

For the first time, he understood what motivated Calder to want to abandon his entire life and stay here. Something existed…he felt it deep down inside…hard to put into words…about just wanting to stay. Storm was the obvious attraction, yes. But he also enjoyed the entire Gallagher clan. He liked the constant, inescapable views of the ocean, but he could live without another dunking. The laid-back, easygoing lifestyle of the residents was welcoming, with the "boy" and "son" names notwithstanding.

Aside from Storm's occasional bout of temper and intrigue, there was virtually no pressure here. No expectations to measure up to, no clients demanding, and no employees expecting something all the time. Much like one would feel during a vacation, except he never took vacations and could only guess at the feelings. And, unless he was mistaken, Calder wasn't going anywhere anytime soon.

Which took him back full circle to, what was he going to do?

He stood and raked a hand through his hair.

The dogs looked up from their beds, eying him.

He could take them back out on the beach. He could go find some food. Maybe another cup of coffee? Yes. That sounded like a good choice now.

He could go for a walk and explore the town. He gave a wry shake of his head. That should take all of what…twenty to thirty minutes?

Fifteen minutes later he strolled along the main street, he wasn't sure of the name, and heading back to River's house. The town was picturesque, almost painfully small, but had great potential. From a developer's eye, he could see so many things that could be done. But based on his conversations with Calder, none of his ideas were ever going to happen. Seems the residents liked their town locked in the past. Okay, fine by him. He still had Atlanta—eventually. Maybe. He shook his head. He'd never felt so messed up in his life.

The sound of a motorcycle pulled him up short. What were the odds of another motorcycle in town? His pulse raced when Storm roared into view, her hair flying. No helmet. Darn crazy woman. He ground his teeth.

She stopped by him, cut the engine, and walked the bike the last few feet. She smiled. "Hi. I was looking for you."

That racing pulse leaped ahead like a runaway horse. "You were? Why?" Another night on the beach, under the moon, and sharing wet kisses?

"Mom sent me to invite you for dinner."

His wild pulse slowed as visions of dancing, firelight, and kisses faded. "Dinner?" he echoed.

"Umm hmmm. She figured with River and Calder gone, you'd be alone, so she said to come eat with us. Raine will be there, too. Bet you anything she's making some special casserole or whatever."

To be honest, he'd not thought that far ahead. River had said dinners from the restaurant in town were in the freezer, but he'd not looked yet. The idea of joining Storm and her family again sounded much more appealing than heating up a frozen dinner. He couldn't stop the smile spreading over his face. "I'd be delighted. What time?"

"Dinner is at five. You can show up any time before that."

"Should I bring something?" A bottle of wine? A dessert? No, Raine was a baker, she'd doubtlessly handle dessert.

She shook her head. "Nope, we've got it all covered. Just bring yourself." She puckered her lips.

He anticipated a kiss. Eagerly, he leaned forward, closing the distance between them. He lowered his eyelids, pulse once more thrumming. The sound of her firing the engine to life made him jump back, eyes wide.

She sent a flirty wink and rolled by. As she swung the bike around and eased past him, she called out a reminder. "By five, Brody." Within seconds, she was gone.

The briny sea air stole her scent away, and Brody was alone on the road. She'd somehow managed to blow out of his life once more. But only for a few hours.

Chapter Thirteen

Storm sat with her parents, Raine, and Brody around the table. She cut a glance over at Brody. He was such a great kisser and had all the suggestions of a being a tender and good lover. When she'd delivered the invitation, she'd wanted to kiss him back, but she also liked shaking him up. He'd expected a kiss, so she forced herself to drive away instead. It'd been hard.

The time they spent out under the stars, in the back of her truck, was enough to excite her and make her hungry for more. After the wedding and her data was safely delivered, she'd see what his plans were. The man lived and died by plans.

She grinned over their raised wineglasses. The subtle vibration of her phone deep in the pockets of her overalls cut her grin short. Oh no, trouble was brewing. "Excuse me," she said, as she lowered her glass and glanced around the table. She slipped around the corner, going to the stairs, and pulled her phone out. *Mark*. Head of her chase team. Her heart beat fast as she considered the few reasons he would call her at home.

"What's up?" She kept her voice low. "Where?" Listening, she debated her options. She asked a few quick questions, made a few statements, and finally issued some orders. She ended the call and heaved a deep breath. She knew not too many options were possible. Next, she needed to plan how to break the news to her family. She turned, colliding with Brody. Air expelled from her chest as she slammed into him.

His hands reached out to steady her.

"What are you doing here?" She pulled herself off his solid chest.

"Listening to your conversation."

She wondered what he was thinking. He stated his confession smoothly, boldly even, without one trace of contrition. Would he hold her again? She remained standing.

Instead he stood like an oak tree.

Irritation rose, and she dropped her hands to her hips. "Just because we had made out earlier does not give you the right to eavesdrop on my private conversations now, McGee."

He shook his head, meeting her verbal challenge. "No, but since I know what a dangerous position you are in, I think I have the right, and obligation, to look out for you."

She snorted, moving aside.

"And since I know how damn difficult it can be getting you to share information," he continued as he trailed her, "I also know it's probably easier just to follow you."

She reached the doorway, spun around, and planted a hand on his chest. "Let me do all the talking," she warned, her voice low.

He nodded and threw in a mock salute, as well.

She huffed, turned back to the dining room, then slid back to her seat.

"Everything all right?" Raine asked.

"Yes. My meteorologist just felt I needed to know about some developments forming near here—

Tennessee and Arkansas. So I thought I'd head down and take a quick look."

Muriel started to protest.

Storm held her hand up. "Wait. I'll be back long before the wedding. Probably in a day or two." She finished her last few bites of dessert and slipped off to pack. She debated if she ought to dig up her research and bring it along but ultimately decided it was safer buried where only she knew about it. She called the airline and booked the soonest flight she could get. In just a few hours, she would be back with her team, back in the field, and away from Brody.

That saddened her. She was enjoying matching herself against him way too much, and their two encounters on the beach had awakened parts of her she had not even remembered. She tried to casually brush it off, but the fact remained she was eager to experience it again. Call it making out or whatever, she wanted to go another round with him, and soon.

She grabbed her packed duffle bag and checked the time. Twelve minutes from Mark's call to fully packed. Not bad. Next, she headed back downstairs to say goodbye. Their long faces made her chuckle. "I'll be back in a couple of days. I am not going far at all," she pacified, looking at the small group. "The issue is probably not even half as serious as my team is thinking it might be."

Her mother pulled her into a hug. "Darling, you be careful and come back safe."

"Of course." She made the rounds, promising to be extra careful and return swiftly so River had nothing to worry about. She hugged and kissed each one. Finally, she shouldered her bag and headed down the steps.

Approaching her SUV, she slid to a halt.

Brody leaned against the bumper, his duffle bag sitting on the hood. Spotting her, he moved to the passenger door, tossed his bag in, and sat inside.

Now she realized he'd been absent from the good-bye lineup. "What do you think you are doing, Brody?" she asked, meeting his silent expression.

"Waiting for you."

She tossed her bag in, her hand curling around the steering wheel and one foot resting on the running board. "I am leaving. Right now. I don't have time for this."

"I know. I'm coming." He pulled on his dark sunglasses and stared ahead, as if to indicate the discussion was closed.

Shock rippled through her. "I'm going to a disaster. One is unfolding now. I have to chase it." She shook her head, wondering if more than just one was unfolding. "I'm heading to the airport now."

Brody sighed. "Wasting time is what you are doing. Do you have a flight number yet?" He pulled out his phone. "Because I don't care if I must ride in the cargo hold down below, woman, I am going. Both on the plane and at the unfolding disaster. Now get in."

She blew out a long breath. He was a bossy cuss. But she didn't have the time or energy to fight over this. Slipping behind the wheel, she grabbed her pink aviator sunglasses and recited her flight number. "Packed and ready to go in under twelve minutes. That's impressive. Aren't you the gypsy?"

Brody snorted. He slid her a sideways look. "Wouldn't you be surprised."

"I hope you packed light," she replied, backing out

the driveway. They hit the road, heading out of town. Storm's mind whirled like the tires on her truck. Brody did realize he'd be flying again, right? She wasn't about to remind him now. Hopefully, he had gum this time.

Surprised? Yes, she was already surprised. She would never have thought he would be this determined to stick with her. But on a chase? This could be dangerous. And he was innocent as to the real risks of storm chasing. And Mark felt this storm could be tricky.

****

Brody shared a seat next to Storm on the plane, where he could keep a careful eye on the other passengers. He gripped the armrests, swallowed hard to quell the roll in his stomach, and silently vowed to keep her safe. Fortunately, she had assured him the flight would be short, and within a couple hours, they would be touching down in Little Rock, where members of her crew promised to be waiting. He discovered he was eager to meet this extended family of hers. Probably as much as she wanted to rejoin them. He easily picked up on her eager cues as she studied the weather on her phone app and texted some guy called Mark.

The plane lurched, and his stomach dropped. The saliva in his mouth turned to cotton. "So, tell me about your team." He was desperate for a distraction.

"You don't like flying, do you?"

"Not really," he said, shaking his head. Pretty soon, he'd need that air-sick bag in front of him. He reached for it three times already and drew his hand back, telling himself he needed to be tougher now or he'd never handle what was ahead once they landed. "Now, about this team of yours?" He had the strong suspicion she knew his question was mostly diversion and only partially curiosity.

She started tapping her finger as she gave names and specialties. "Nate is my navigator. He could guide us into a rabbit's burrow and back out the exit route. Doug and Dave are my resident drivers. They drive alongside the twisters like they were choo-choo trains and keep it steady. Rain, hail, lightning— nothing makes them break into a sweat. Phil is my photographer, and Virg does the videotaping. They will brave anything to shoot whatever footage we need. They could tell you war stories to make your hair stand on end. Mark is my resident meteorologist, the senior severe weather expert. He can read the signs better than I can, and I'd trust his instincts all the way to anywhere. I think he's part rain man or something. Wade, Clay, Morg, and Mace are the science guys. They have their specialties, unique set of skills, and have a nose for weather. And last is Raul, the radio guy. Cell phones don't always work where we go, so his ham radio keeps us in touch and can spread warnings out ahead of our position."

All guys, he noted, and he'd bet they were all under the control of her little pinkie, if they were smart guys. They would be spared her wrath if they stayed there. He knew when he decided to come along as her chaperon, he might earn another round of her temper. He considered other options first. Yes, it would have been easier just to follow her, book the next flight, and remain in the shadows. But he felt just joining her was safer and certainly more pleasurable. At least, she couldn't push him out of a moving plane. He wasn't under the control of her pinkie and had no intentions to be so, but he wasn't stupid, either.

But a woman like Storm having a group of men flocking to her like bees to honey and do her bidding was logical. Hopefully, they could also keep her safe. With eleven guys, twelve including himself, she ought to be plenty safe. Well, at least from the people interested in her research. He couldn't do much to stop a weather event. "Storm, I have to ask, what did you do with your research?" He leaned in to keep his voice low. Surely, she didn't bring it along? If she had, he wanted to know about it.

She hesitated, glancing from his intent expression to the seat rest in front of her.

No one around them appeared to be listening to their conversation. The mother and toddler behind them were singing a happy song, and the college kids across from them were engrossed in their tablets, laughing, and sharing whatever they displayed. To judge from the stands of music filtering across the aisle, he'd bet they were watching music videos. "Storm. I need to know where we stand."

She pulled her hair back. "I left it behind." She met his gaze.

He smiled, and the look of relief on her face probably matched the one on his. He pried his fingers off the armrest long enough to pat her hand. "I know you don't have to care what I think, but that was a good decision. And I'm glad you can share that information."

She grinned and began rambling, sharing anecdotes and adventures about her team.

Probably to help ease his obvious flight phobias. He relaxed; his breathing smoothed out as he felt himself drawn into her stories.

Suddenly, she stopped and fixed him with a somber gaze, her eyes wide.

His heart stalled. "Storm?"

She blinked. "You know, I have never been able to share this kind of stuff with anyone outside my team, not even with my own family." She paused. "Thank you for caring about what's important in my life."

His pulse raced ahead, and he felt both warm inside and cold. Her honest comment scared him. That she felt safe to share that stuff, most of which he did not understand, was great. Her sharing put something between them he didn't know what to think of. Like a silken cord, it was both strong and fragile, and he was scared to touch what lay between them.

"Brody, do you have any idea of what you just signed yourself up for?"

Her question, barely above a whisper, shook him from his thoughts. Was she referring to the airplane ride, the monster weather that awaited them, or the ties that now bound them? No, he didn't think he knew much of anything right then. "Sure. Of course." He bluffed. "Do you think you're the only one who can color outside the lines?"

"I guess not. You're starting to surprise me."

He grinned, joy rising at her compliment. "Your team all sound like decent, reasonable-minded, and intelligent men."

"They are. And most are married and fathers. A couple have steady girlfriends. A few of them are grandpas. They all hold jobs outside of the chase season. They are all excellent and extremely knowledgeable about what they do."

"That's great. But can they also keep you safe?"

He sure planned to keep her away from danger. He heard the pride in her voice of her team, but he intended to do his part.

"Safe from what?"

What was unclear about his question? "From those individuals after your work."

"These guys are my work team. They are not my babysitters."

He eyed her drumming fingers and thinned lips. Somehow, his innocent question crossed a line.

Three hours later, the plane flew out of the turbulence and landed without incident. Vastly relieved, Brody considered dropping to the ground and give it a quick kiss, then reconsidered when he recalled Storm's electrifying kiss the last time they flew together. He considered the option of demanding another one from her upon disembarking but decided against that, too. Just in case they were being followed, he needed to keep his senses alert. Storm's kisses had a way of sending his senses into another time zone.

Just like the time they spent on the beach—was that only a few hours ago? He about died when she stuck her finger in her mouth to avoid answering his questions. He could think of much better things to do with that mouth. When she twirled her hair in a sudden case of nerves, he knew he could handle her hair much better. And he'd been right. That hair, those eyes, her lips, and that independent streak a mile wide nearly made him forget the questions he set out to find answers to.

Now, away from the relative safety of Sweetwater Harbor, he needed to keep all his wits about him. He carefully looked around before he grabbed his bag and followed her off the plane.

She stopped and searched the crowd of waiting people.

A man in a white polo shirt and jeans called her name and waved.

"Mark," she greeted, rushing into his arms for a quick hug. "Nice to see you again."

Brody witnessed the brief exchange and a bolt of something hot sliced through Brody. Tamping it down, he reminded himself they were co-workers and part of a team. The hug meant nothing. Right? Stoutly, he sized the guy up.

Mark was about five feet, eight inches tall, easily in his sixties, sporting a smiling face full of wrinkles, and a full head of gray hair. His friendly blue eyes sparkled as he released Storm, and his athletic build reminded Brody of a man one third his age. This man would also be the senior severe weather expert, the rain man Storm trusted so well.

"Mark, this is Brody; he is a friend of mine," Storm introduced the men.

"Brody, nice to meet you." Mark extended his hand. "A friend?"

Brody felt surprised at the older man's sure grip. "My business partner and best friend is marrying Storm's sister," Brody explained. He found himself liking how she referred to him as a friend. Several other terms might have been chosen instead.

Mark nodded. "Ah, we'll try to wrap this weather up so you two will be back in time for River's wedding." He chuckled. "Muriel and Cordell would never let us live it down if we kept Storm out here too long."

Brody was impressed with how familiar Mark was with the family…by description, at least. Had he ever traveled to meet them in that small Carolina town? He almost asked, but Storm and Mark were already in motion. He trotted to keep up.

They made their way out into the humid air of the Arkansas parking lot.

Brody followed them to a large white van. Antennas whipped in the faint breeze, and decals peppered the van's exterior. Brody tried to decipher them but gave up as the sliding door opened. He spotted more men inside, seated at tables and hunched over laptops. Computer screens lined the wall of the van. Hearing Mark's call, they scurried out, pulling Storm into quick hugs of welcome.

"Brody, meet Dave and Clay. Guys, meet my friend, Brody."

A driver and one of the science guys, Brody recalled. One in his forties and one around his late twenties. Handshakes were done, and talk swiftly turned to the weather and the important storm they left Carolina to come chase. Staring at the images moving across the laptop screens, Brody realized he understood nothing of what they were discussing, except it was going to be big. Casting a glance at the bright sky overhead, noticing how it conflicted with the images on their computers, he wondered what he was getting into.

****

Riding shotgun next to Storm, Brody watched the landscape change as they left Little Rock and drove southwest. Overhead, the high feathery clouds of white curls gave way to lower banks of gray. Soon, they rolled the windows up against the cooling air.

Eventually, a few drops of rain splattered the windshield.

Storm cut him a broad smile. "Are you ready for some fun?" she asked.

Caught between a sense of trepidation and the fact he wished her eyes danced with delight for him, he nodded. "Of course. I have seen the movie *Twister,* you know."

Storm laughed outright, amused. She patted his arm. "Brody, I have lived *Twister.*"

Dave, the driver, chuckled softly and kept his gaze on the road.

They reached a community park at the edge of some new town. The rain had stopped. Another large van and two sport utility vehicles with spare gas cans strapped to the rears formed a semi-circle. Men lounged about, reading computer screens, smoking, and waiting. As they pulled up, the men all snapped to attention like a precision military troop. Brody was impressed.

More introductions and handshakes were done around the circle.

Storm studied the data, listening to her guys as they explained their findings.

Brody stood behind her as he took in all the sights and sounds. While he understood little of what they talked about, he knew something big was expected, and soon, Storm and her team were excited. Whatever supercells were, this group wanted to see them.

Finally, Storm whirled, blush in her cheeks as she pointed fingers toward the men. "Okay, Dave and Doug, take the vans. Nate, you guide us in the SUV. I'll take Brody with the other SUV. Let's roll."

They scrambled for their vehicles, each man

jumping in and going to work. Doors slammed. Engines fired. Headlights shone.

Brody tightened his seat belt, his heart already hammering. Was it because he and Storm were alone in a car, or because she was about to drive them straight into a tornado? "So, now what?" He stared at the darker clouds overhead.

"Now, we drive toward the action. We're headed to where the radars show the most activity in wind, temperature, things like that."

He did not trust his voice, so he nodded instead.

"Just how much do you know about weather?"

He looked over. "I can tell when it's sunny or raining outside."

She laughed, a full-bodied amusement. "Umm, you might learn a little more today. Let's just hope you can handle rough weather in a car better than you handled the airplane rides."

He was sunk. What a shame he hadn't had time to get more motion sickness gum.

The random rain drops they experienced outside Little Rock grew into a steady rainfall. Storm flipped on the wiper blades. The silence in the vehicle was deafening, saved only by the splatter of rain and the wiper blades.

"No radio?" He gestured toward the dash and reached for the knob. "I can find us something.

She quickly shook her head. "Never on a hot chase. I need to hear what Raul and the others are saying, and I can't if we're headbanging along to the Grateful Dead. Sorry."

He turned his attention back to the thickening clouds. Grateful Dead? Was that her choice in music?

Or a passing pun at their current endeavor? He'd no idea clouds could get so thick and dark. He couldn't even think what they reminded him of now. They passed cottony soft clouds several miles ago. He looked at the line of vehicles they made, headlights shining and antennas waving. A caravan of gypsies, restless people who chased storms for the thrill and…

"So, tell me why you don't believe in love."

"Huh?" He blinked, surprised at the sudden question. Pulling his attention off the caravan and the developing weather beyond the window, he regarded her, remembering a dunk in the ocean that started out with a comment like that one. "Who said I don't?"

"Calder did. Well, it was River actually, quoting what Calder cited you as saying."

He shot her a quick grin. "So, a quote of a quote of my quote? Well, nothing can possibly get misconstrued that way, could it?" He grinned at his dry humor. Sometimes, he fell into situations where his sardonic wit came out.

She smiled. "Maybe, maybe not. You appear to view love as a two-edged sword that cuts deep and bleeds hard."

He winced. "Ouch! That sounds awfully harsh, not to mention painful. Someone would have to have been ripped to shreds by love to think that way."

"Okay, so tell me what it was you really said."

He watched the windshield wipers slapping in unison. "I believe those misquoted quotes began as a conversation Calder and I had about the time he wanted to propose to that socialite, Penelope Jordon. I simply said I would honor his wishes, but I had no desires of my own to join with someone and follow him down the aisle anytime soon." He grinned. "No double-edged sword or deep cuts."

She grinned. "So, you don't believe in love."

"I did not say that, Storm. There is a difference. And there are many forms of love."

"Yes, I've studied them. Which ones in particular are you opposed to?"

He shook his head. "None, actually. I was merely saying to Calder I do not believe in the institution of love and marriage. People are too quick to confuse another form of love with true, lasting agape love. They rush to declare love and affection with wild abandon when it is simply Eros or a physical love at best. So, they hasten into marriage based on emotions and one day realize they have no lasting emotions left. Then they immediately dash to the divorce courts." He paused for a breath. "If people would have taken things in slower steps and tried to understand what they were truly feeling, a lot of time, emotion and money would be spared."

"Ouch, that sounds kind of harsh there, McGee."

"People conduct studies to see what various odds are of staying married and what can increase the odds of divorce." He shrugged. "That sounds like reality."

She tossed him a smile. "So, you love nothing at all? Sunsets? Peanut butter? Puppy kisses? Satin sheets? Your parents?"

He curled his hands into fists. She had a way to make a simple conversation complicated. "I did not say that. I love lots of things and people. I just prefer to identify what sort of love I hold for each item and person."

She tapped her fingers along the wheel, humming

softly. Finally she looked over. "How calculating. How logical. Where is your emotion at?"

He felt as if she slapped him. "I have plenty of emotions. Just because I don't let them run rampant without restraint doesn't mean I have no emotions."

She grinned. "Are you saying I have no restraint?"

Moments have occurred, but he felt it better not to bring them up. "You could do with a bit more," he acknowledged, breath held and rigid as he waited to see her reaction.

She laughed. "Maybe," she agreed. "I have been told that once or twice before." She took one hand off the wheel to count three, four, and five on her fingers. "Since before I started school actually." She paused, shooting him a playful grin. "And I love eating peanut butter cookies in bed. So, what kind of love is that, McGee?"

"Eros, the physical kind," he replied almost automatically. He didn't doubt what she said for a moment. She was Storm, and nothing was going to change her. And now he was out here in the relative no-man's-land, chasing a killer storm with her. To keep her safe. Of her list of loves, he wondered what topped her list? Satin sheets and peanut butter cookies? Pictures took flight in his mind. Turning to the weather, he tried to shake them off.

Suddenly, the black clouds they had been driving toward caught his eye. One dipped down, forming a cylinder shape as it stretched from the cloud toward the ground. His chest compressed, he couldn't breathe, and he gripped the dashboard. "Oh my! Is that a tornado?"

Chapter Fourteen

Storm eagerly scanned the sky, craning her neck to see what got him excited. Had she missed something? Spotting nothing in the form or promise of a tornado, she surveyed the clouds as he might be seeing them. Ah, there it was. The wall cloud at ten o'clock. She supposed it could resemble the vortex of a tornado. If it were spinning, which this one was not, of course. Given time, this might dip down, spin around, and work itself into a nice little twister. But not right now. She swallowed a sigh. "No, that would be a cloud."

"Oh."

She tried to hide her smile at his letdown. She snuck a peek and noticed the relief in his face. His white-knuckled grip on the dash lessened ever so slightly as he continued to scan the sky.

"Disappointed?"

"No. Yes. I don't know." He shook his head and met her glance. "I'd just expected to see tornados, probably lots of them, and fairly soon." He pried his hand off long enough to flick a wrist past the windshield. "Guess that proves I'm not ready for this."

No one ever was. She remembered her first few chases. She'd been equal parts scared and excited. "You don't get out much, do you?"

"Out?"

"Yeah, like out of doors, out of town, or out of

your shell." As soon as she spoke, she saw the sting of surprise cross his face.

"We have clouds in Atlanta."

The defensiveness in his tone couldn't be mistaken. She'd insulted him. "Yeah, but do you ever just stop and stare at them? When was the last time you sat and watched the rain fall?"

"I don't recall offhand, though I suspect I shall be shortly."

She chuckled. "Or we might just do a bunch of extreme sitting and endless driving," she pointed out. "And end up with nothing."

"I doubt that for two reasons. One, all you highly trained people seem too convinced and too intense for this to be a wild goose chase. And second, any time spent in your company is quickly getting to be not only hard on my heart but pleasurable, as well."

She inhaled sharply, warmth touching her cheeks. How could Brody make her blush and giggle? She thought hard for a response. "Yep, you're probably right."

The sky turned a darker shade, clouds blotted out the sun, and still they drove into the heavier rain.

"Bored yet?" Storm asked finally as she drummed the steering wheel.

"Not even close." He laughed. Turning from the darkening scene outside, he regarded her a moment. "Why storm chasing? I get the impression someone like you could have done just about anything."

"Thanks, but I know what I am," she finally answered. "And what I am not, which is more important."

"What you're not?"

She nodded, glancing at the sky and then over to him. "I know I am not organized like River or great with figures and having a head for business like Raine is. I can't make schedules and meet deadlines like River. I am not disciplined enough for the military like Winter. With the grades I got in school, everyone knew I never cheated on tests." She giggled as she wrinkled her nose in a smile.

"So, what are you, Storm?"

She nodded toward the view ahead. "I am wild and free, like the weather." She turned, a sadness in her eyes. "Can you even hope to keep up with me, Brody McGee?"

He opened his mouth to immediately answer and closed it without speaking. He paused, glancing outside, then down to his shoes on the floorboards. A muscle ticked in his jaw. "I think I can."

Well, that was something. She'd see how he made it through the next few hours. They rode on, with her focusing on the intel her team shared and the increasing weather unfolding before her. Having Brody riding shotgun and sharing this adventure pleased her.

"Can I ask you a couple weather questions? Things I've wondered about."

That surprised her. He'd wondered about weather? "Shoot."

"Is it true the tree leaves turn upside down before it rains?"

She was amused at his subject and chuckled. "It's true. There are two reasons why leaves might flip over. One is the wind. Gusty winds usually precede rain"—she waved out the window at the increasing raindrops slapping the windshield—"which cause leaves to slip over, or upside down. And sometimes it will be windy, without the rain, so that's not a given weather tracker. And humidity is the other reason. The humid air around rainstorms softens the leaves, so they might hang in a flipped position or move easier in a breeze."

Brody stroked his chin. "Fascinating. Okay, what about the red sky sailor thing?"

Storm furrowed her brow, thinking. "Ah, yes. Red sky at night, sailor's delight, red sky in the morning, sailors take warning. That has been around for centuries." She waved a hand in a circle in the air before returning it to the wheel. "The different colors we see up there have to do with wavelengths. The sunlight bounces off the water vapor as it passes through the atmosphere. There they separate into the colors of the spectrum. Red indicates the clouds have lots of moisture and dust. Now, if the sky is red at sunset, it's because of high levels of pressure and stable air from the west. Since from the west is the direction our weather normally moves in, a red sunset represents good weather. However, red sunrises usually mean dust particles from a storm have moved from the west, going east. A deep red sky could suggest heavy rains due to a high concentration of water in the clouds."

****

Brody smiled. He enjoyed the peeks he stole of her profile and her relaxed expression as she talked about weather. Most of her technical stuff bounced through his brain and disappeared, but he realized this was something Storm was both passionate and knowledgeable about. The weather outside their windows worsened, but she waxed on about clouds, rain, and moisture. He marveled at her dedication. What would it feel like to be that passionate about something? He'd never felt that for anything in his life, and now he wondered why not. What had he been missing?

The rain intensified, until the vehicles in front became lost in the sheets of rain. He watched Storm tightened her grip on the wheel as the roads grew slick, and the car in front left sliding tracks on the rain-soaked road. Hail pounded the windshield, making him jump at each slap. Lightning crashed across the skies, and Brody jerked ramrod straight, his jaw so tight it hurt.

The winds tossed tree branches, and whipped them so wildly, he was amazed they didn't all break off. Clumps of leaves and small branches spiraled across the road like tumbleweeds. Thunder cracked, and he inhaled sharply, his palm going to his chest. He frowned. He'd heard thunder lots of times, why the cold chills and flinching now?

Lightning zigzagged, illuminating the sky in a crooked ripple of light in front of their vehicle. Brody was sure his heart stopped. Close? No, that lightning was right on top of them! His fingernails clawed into the dash.

"It's going to get worse. Sure you're up for this?"

He could have almost laughed at her soft question. Of course, he wasn't. He was already scared witless. And this was just the beginning? But to jump out now was unthinkable. He was bound to see this through now. "Of course I am," he replied stoutly.

"I just want to warn you...this could be a wild ride."

He coughed, trying to force the thick lump in his throat that refused to budge. So far, everything with

Storm has been a wild ride. How much worse could chasing a real tornado really be?

She grinned.

The chunks of hail grew larger, whacking the windshield like pellets from a gun. One cracked the windshield between them, making them both flinch. The crack grew, like strands of a spider's web. Brody pressed his palm against the cool glass.

Stranded motorists stalled beside the road, their red flashing hazard lights barely visible through the onslaught.

His heart thumped painfully against his chest. Was he going to die?

"Flash flooding is a big problem now."

Brody nodded, his voice now gone. Wouldn't flash flooding be only one of the big problems now? What he could see of the clouds was nothing but a swirl of darkening layers, going from dark grey to black…ominous black.

Noise crackled through the radio, and Storm hastened to respond.

He understood nothing of their language.

"Okay." She turned to Brody, her eyes dark and shiny. "Get ready. We're going into the bear's cage."

He gulped. "B-b-bear's c-c-cage?"

"Yeah, pretty much what it sounds like. Sort of like entering the cage of a wild bear and locking yourself in. Radar picked up some funnel activity less than a mile ahead."

His heartrate picked up speed, and his breath caught. Nausea clawed at his throat. His head swam with the fact he was really doing this. The crack in the window before him was all the proof he needed to tell himself he must make an appointment with a psychiatrist once he returned to Atlanta. If he returned to Atlanta. Absolutely nothing was normal about any of this.

She reached down to the console and plucked up a tube of lip gloss.

He watched as she casually rolled it on her lips.

She recapped the tube and began returning it to its spot.

It slipped, and he grabbed for it. Their hands touched, and he met her eye. His heart spiraled.

She pursed her lips, wetting the glossy shine.

He wondered how she could look so sexy and desirable as they were about to face death in the eye.

She punched the gas, following the blurry taillights of the vans in front of them, her attention fixed on the water-washed road, twisting tire tracks, and the driving hail.

Brody stared through the cracked glass in speechless shock. Power lines toppled over, lying bent like toothpicks. Wires flipped and writhed like giant serpents, and sparks flew. Branches snapped off trees, lying like discarded litter caught in the wind. Cars lay on the road, on the side of the road, on the median, and flipped on sides and backs like giant beetles. Brody felt his jaw drop in utter disbelief. What…

"A small one already tore through here. Raul's radioed the town ahead to send patrols out to check on those," she said, nodding to the upturned cars. "Hopefully, everyone got out ahead and are all safe somewhere."

Small one? And it overturned cars and snapped power line poles? So, what could a big tornado overturn? He didn't even want to think about it. Instead, he took the moment to appreciate her clear concern for others and for strangers.

They crossed railroad tracks, and he saw two things simultaneously. First, he saw a string of three train cars, parked on the tracks in the distance. Second, he noticed what could only be a huge, dark, swirling tornado slicing through the landscape ahead. He mustered every ounce of control not to jerk the wheel from Storm and spin them away from the whirling beast they were racing toward. Bear's cage. Yes, now he understood the phrase. He felt like they were facing off against a giant, rabid grizzly bear.

He watched, oddly fixated as the tornado churned along, picked up the three railway cars, and swept them into its black mass. Before he could draw another stunned breath, they dropped, literally from the sky to crash several feet from where they stood parked on the tracks only moments before.

"Oh. My. Word," he said, each sound an effort. "They were lifted and tossed like they were no more than a child's toy." He studied the spinning funnel with a fresh appreciation for its raw strength…its violence. How much had those now-mangled railway cars weighed? Tons.

"Yeah, that was pretty impressive."

"Impressive?" he parroted, wondering if he needed to thump his chest to get his heart beating again. "My God, woman, it was fantastic. Unbelievable. Inconceivable."

She shot him a smile. The radio crackled again, and she picked it up.

She talked with what sounded to Brody as a foreign

language. More weather terminology. Gaze glued to the twisting tornado, he waited, heart hammering. At least the hail had decreased a little. That would be good, right?

"More funnels ahead. They're heading for some town called Peony."

He swallowed, hopes dashed that he'd seen all the violence and destruction there was going to be. "Is that where we're going?"

"Of course. Look, there's a twin." She pointed farther on the horizon.

Through the flying debris and rain, he spotted a smaller swirling mass. Two of them? His mouth went dry. The wall cloud quickly formed a perfectly rotating cylinder, stretching for the ground. The town of Peony spilled into view beneath the ominous black sky. Already, people stopped their cars, abandoning them everywhere and jumping out with arms waving and screaming.

Brody understood. He felt their panic. He wanted to do the same.

Trees toppled, lightning streaked through the sky, debris flew—he didn't know where to look next. He swiveled as much as he could within the confines of his seat belt.

Streetlights fell, caught in the wind, sending sparks arcing into the darkness. Brody marveled how it could be so dark and still so light at the same time. Dark enough to need headlights and see flying embers of arcing fire, yet light enough to see debris swirling in the wind. Larger tree limbs broke off, and entire trees bent, snapping in two.

In spite of the terror gripping him, he was still

acutely aware of Storm's amused grin as she navigated the hazardous road. She spoke into the radio.

She seemed oblivious to the destruction surrounding them. Yet, that was the reason they were here.

"Wade says these winds are topping out at over eighty miles an hour. That's a good indicator."

"Of what?"

She smiled.

The gesture was as if she patronized him and his fear and his ignorance. Right now, he wasn't too proud to deny either. He'd never been so scared in his life.

"Of more activity. This is a gust front. See? Our twin funnel is working itself into quite a state."

How had he managed to forget the twin funnel? Perhaps because he was caught up in the destruction before him and the chaos spread out. He turned and watched the spinning column work its way into town with a morbid fascination. It took down signs and power lines and picked up chunks of whatever was in its path. Mesmerized, he watched as it spit the chunks back out as broken debris.

"Do you hear that?"

All he heard was what sounded like a locomotive racing on and the screams of the terrified. And his own thundering pulse. "Bedlam? Yes, I hear it."

She chuckled. "I'm glad you still have a sense of humor, but no, I meant the sirens. No sirens were blaring warnings."

"And the significance of that would be?"

"Part of the work early storm chasers have done was the ability to call and warn cities when tornados were heading their way. At least five minutes ago, Raul called ahead to Peony to alert them. Emergency personnel could then sound the sirens, alerting citizens to take shelter. They should have more people in shelters, less out here, and sirens should be blaring."

It made sense. Anyone in their right mind would want to escape this pandemonium as fast as possible. Okay, so what did that say about him right now? That he was enjoying the marvelous spectacles around them bothered him. It was almost as if Storm's joy was contagious, spreading over to him. "Maybe someone freaked and took off, forgetting to start the sirens?"

Storm shook her head. "Nope. They would never have someone in that sort of position who would panic and do something like that. Emergency workers need to have a certain degree of tolerance to emergencies without flipping out."

Okay, rule that out as a possible pick of career choices. In emergencies, he defaulted to panic mode. His racing heart and death grip on the dash were proof enough.

Their caravan slowed as they cruised through town. The rain was decreased to drizzle. Not sure what to think anymore, Brody simply stared out the window, rocked by the raw destruction.

Beyond the toppled trees, broken buildings, arcing power lines, and debris piles, he saw smashed cars and rain-washed streets running with mud. A few patches of road exploded in a crumbled mess of asphalt. People stood, huddled in crying masses or rushing alone, searching through piles of rubble, their faces twisted into lines of misery and fear. Tears streaked down their dirty faces.

The place looked like it was from a war movie. He

forced his gaze back inside to look over at Storm's reaction. Storm shook her head from side to side, mumbling under her breath.

Fire engines and police cars swept through the streets, stopping at intervals, with lights rotating in swirling colors, blending with the rain.

"Oh, look!" Storm slammed on the brakes.

He slumped forward against the seat belt. Before he could determine what caused her action, he heard the door unlatch.

She got out of the car, sprinting toward a young boy standing alone in the middle of the street.

Quickly, he followed her, immediately slapped by the eerie silence surrounding the town, despite the cries and running people. Chills slithered up his spine as he approached Storm.

The little boy cried, tears racing down his mud-streaked face. His hair was mussed, and, in his hands, he clutched a stuffed toy. "Mama! Mama!" he wailed, turning in a tiny circle. "Mama!"

Storm fell to her knees, taking his dirty, wet body to her chest. Cradling him, she smoothed his hair. "It's okay, sweetie. We'll find your mama. What's your name, honey?"

He sniffled a couple times, looking up at Brody, who stood rooted next to a broken section of street. "I'm Robbie."

"Robbie, I'm Storm. And this tall guy is Brody, and we're here to help find your mama, okay?

Robbie nodded, sniffling again.

Storm pulled him back at arm's length, a big smile on her face. "How old are you, Robbie?"

"Five."

"Oh wow. Marvelous. Five is a wonderful age to be. I loved being five. What do you have there in your hand?"

"My race car." He opened his palm, showing his yellow stuffed race car, with a number seven decal stuck to the side and a smiley face sewn on the front.

"Hey, that's a really cool car, Robbie. Now, where were you and your mama at just before the storm came?"

Brody listened, amazed that even as they were surrounded by rubble and debris and chaos in the eerie quiet, she was taking time to soothe and help a frightened child. He found himself just as captivated by the fearless Storm who drove hell-bent through a storm, chasing a rogue series of tornados, and the compassionate Storm who comforted a scared five-year-old boy.

She took Robbie's hand into hers, and they began walking the broken streets, sidestepping piles of rubble and puddles of rain.

Brody followed, half expecting a movie director to jump out any second from an upturned car and shout *Cut!*

They approached a house that looked like it had been bombed, with upturned trees on the car in the drive and on the roof. Remains of a tire swing poked through the branches of a tree.

Robbie stopped, fresh sobs shaking him.

Two police cars blocked the street, shadowed by a fire truck. Men in uniforms cloistered around the fallen house.

"I have the little boy who lives there," Storm called out, pointing to the house. "He lost his mother."

One man turned to her, sizing up both her and the child. "In here," he gestured grimly to what was left of the house.

She nodded, spinning around, and taking Robbie once more to her chest. She murmured words of encouragement.

Soon, he giggled.

She laughed.

Next, he was showing her something to do with his race car.

Brody divided his attention from Storm to the workers, and he put the pieces together. Once he got it, his heart squeezed. She was diverting Robbie's attention from his damaged home and his buried mother so the men could dig her out. Her courage and tenderness, a total contrast from the Storm he knew, confounded him, and touched him.

From where he stood, the blue lights revolving from the nearby police car cast an almost angelic halo glowing over her, knocking at his heart. He staggered under the weight of the realization, like a hand slap to the back of his head. Clearly, he saw the colors and truths that Storm brought to his dull life. Now, he saw through a new colored lens, and it both frightened and exhilarated him.

More shouts drew his attention back up the street where some of the members of her team raced up, dragging some strange object. She glanced, nodded, and continued in some story she and Robbie were sharing.

The team took the object to the collapsed house and joined with the police and fire workers.

Soon, a young woman was helped from the rubble. "Robbie!" she sobbed and reached her arms out.

Storm rushed him over.

The young mother eagerly swept her son into her arms.

The warm embrace brought tears to Brody's eyes. Brushing them away, he blinked at the tender scene of mother and child reunited because of the efforts of Storm and her team.

Turning, Storm returned to Brody, a satisfied smile on her face. She clasped him on the shoulder. "Come on, there're more survivors out there to find. We've got the technology to find them, and we need to help this town."

Torn between the newfound admiration in Storm and remnants of his residual panic, Brody followed her and the team members as they went from search party to search party, lending their hearts and talents in finding missing family members and even two hissing cats and one grateful lost, old dog. Amid shouts and cries, the work was brutal, sweaty, and miserable. But the reunions were joyous.

Emotions Brody never felt awakened from somewhere deep inside his soul, making him push past the mess and blood and unpleasant tasks to roll up his sleeves and help find the lost. The tears that rolled down his own cheeks as families were united warmed his heart like nothing he'd ever experienced.

Stopping at last, Storm heaved a sigh, massaging her back. "I think we're done. This town of Peony will survive to rebuild again, and so will its people."

Brody looked around, taking in both the destruction and the joyous families, still amazed. "I can't believe we lived through all this."

Storm grabbed him, hauling him close.

He only had time to grunt in surprise before she pressed her lips to his, hands reaching for his waist. Just as his scattered wits registered her mind-blowing kiss, he felt her moving away.

She smiled wickedly and rocked back on the balls of her feet. "There's that mouth to mouth I promised you a while back."

He groaned, licking his lips. "Woman, you might be easy on the eyes, but you sure are a devil on a man's heart."

She grinned, suddenly coy. "Do you need more mouth to mouth?"

Did he? He sure wanted more. But first, he needed to reconcile these two Storms. The wild one was emerging now that the threat was over. But her courage and compassion remained. Now, he was starting to see what her storm chasing was. It wasn't just driving fast for the thrills, challenging nature's fury. Her work was to help others through research, learning, and personal risk. For all the Robbies and their parents who had not survived before, she was working, along with her team, to help ensure future people would make it.

Looking at her demure smile, her eyes dancing in anticipation and her glossy lips, he had never seen anything so perfect and wild before. The swirling blue police lights made a twirling angel halo around her. His throat convulsed, and his heart raced once again. Oh yeah, he wanted more mouth to mouth, and lots of it. About to move in to claim some, he noticed something that checked him. "In a minute maybe," he murmured. "But look there." He pointed to where her shirt had been ripped on a piece of fallen steel as she had worked to pull a person out from under it earlier. Now, he spotted multiple streaks of red. "You're bleeding."

"What?" She whipped around, hands going to the tear in her shirt. Staring at the gashes, she turned up with her eyes wide, the color draining from her face. "Oh no," she murmured a second before slumping into his arms.

Shocked, he gripped her gently, taking her soft, relaxed body into his grip. What just happened?

Chapter Fifteen

Astonished, Brody grabbed Storm and eased her out along the ground. He checked for a pulse like he'd seen the firemen do, and his fear drained away when he felt the strong throbbing beneath his trembling fingertips. Fearless Storm fainted at the sight of blood? But they had both seen lots of blood today.

Gently sweeping her tangled hair out of the way, he spent a moment to take in the serene look of her at total rest. Her stillness both awed and scared him. Next, he gently pulled her shirt up, exposing the wound. The gash was shallow, but as wide as his pinkie finger. He pulled the fabric farther back, and his heart thumped faster as he spotted the edge of her tattoo, the one that had eluded him for so long and tormented his imagination.

His curiosity overrode propriety, and he lifted enough shirt away to see it clearly, feeling his brows pulling into a puzzled frown. A black barcode stared back, except under the code, instead of numbers he saw letters. He spelled them out. *I-A-M-N-O-T-O-W-N-E-D.*

Working the letters into words, he looked out across the rubble strewn horizon, wheels turning. Spotting Mark, he hailed him over, quickly pulling her shirt back into place. "She's got a few cuts, probably caused by that beam from that one house," he spoke as he continued examining Storm. "Do you have anything handy to clean it up?"

Mark studied the wound. "Yeah, she won't need stitches. Good cleaning and big bandage will do her." He chuckled. "Girl never could handle seeing her own blood. Show her a severed stump spewing blood by the gallon, and she's unfazed. Show her a paper cut on her own finger, and she hits the floor."

Brody fought the impulse to grin at Mark's fond words. They only added to her charm and beauty. Storm was Storm, and he didn't think he'd want her any other way.

"Be right back," Mark promised.

Within minutes, he was back with a small first aid kit. "If you got this, I need to go help the others."

Brody waved him away, already digging through the kit for disinfectant. "I'm good. Thanks." Glad she would not feel the sting, he rushed to clean and bandage the wound. As he was repacking the kit, he heard a sound.

She moaned. "Oh no, what happened?"

"You fainted."

"Darn."

"Beautiful," he corrected, earning her frown.

She sat up, hands exploring the wound.

He swatted her hands away. "Don't be messing up my doctoring skills." He held her hands, staring into her blue-green eyes. "Just let me look at you."

"Why?"

Why? He struggled to put words to his emotions. He witnessed her spice, her courage, and her compassion to others. He'd been alongside to see her bravery. And now, he saw her vulnerability. They all blended together to create one tantalizing woman. How could he express that? He hitched his shoulder. "Because I want to look at you. You're beautiful and wonderful, Storm Diana."

A blush colored her cheeks. "Well, now you know my worse secret."

"I do? What's that?"

"I faint at blood."

"Isn't it just at your own? And don't worry. I think it's a very enthralling attribute." He also adored her subdued expression.

She snorted. "It's unprofessional and for sissies."

He wagged his head. Her restraint hadn't lasted long. "I disagree. But either way, tell me about the bar code."

She inhaled sharply, and her eyes rounded. Then they narrowed in suspicion. "Do I have an inch of me you haven't examined?"

"Lots of them, and maybe later I can see more. The barcode?"

She gave him a rakish grin. She climbed to her feet and pushed aside his effort to assist. "There might be something on you I want to see later."

"Doubtlessly." Once more, her sass warmed his heart. He knew she was fully on the mend. "Barcode, Storm."

Her huff could have been heard across the remains of town.

"Okay, it's just what it means. I am not owned."

"By?"

"Anyone. We are a people of followers who are nothing more than a number. A driver's license number, a social security number, an employee or educational or military identification number, credit rating—you name it. Everywhere we go, we are only a number. We are defined by a number of some sort now, instead of our name or of who we are. We are stamped with a barcode of what defines us now. My statement is just that. I am not owned by anyone, nor am I defined by a number assigned by someone else."

He considered that, loudly hearing the ring of truth. "But you have many of those numbers. A driver's license, social security, and so forth." How did she reconcile the inescapable fact of life?

She scowled. "I have them, but I refuse to be defined or owned by them."

"You know what?" he began slowly as he eyed her up and down, thoughts churning through his mind and heart. "I might have to reevaluate my thoughts on lasting love."

"Really?" She smiled as he pulled her in and held her close. "Because of me?"

"Yes." He expelled a breath. He wasn't surprised to find himself still shaking now that they were both standing. He swung his gaze around the chaos surrounding them and rested it back on her lovely blue-green eyes. "I've seen some incredible things and felt some unbelievable things in the last day. It will all need further research." He might live for his facts and figures, but after what he had witnessed and heard, he was thinking maybe he also needed to live for someone else.

She moved in close, nuzzling his ear. "A possible marriage?"

"I'm not sure on that yet," he admitted, shivering as her tongue trailed over his ear. "But the forecast is looking favorable."

Darting the tip of her tongue into his ear, she giggled at the tremors shaking him. "Winter ought to be arriving home soon. Why don't we go back now?"

"Right now?" They were in the middle of a town literally reduced to ruins.

She nodded. "The information we gleaned on this one chase will keep everyone on the team busy for a while."

He grabbed her and swirled around, taking her in a circle as she flung her arms out, laughing. Wearing the biggest smile, he deposited her back on the ground. "Let's go. I can't wait to meet your brother."

****

The loose ends were tied up, the flight back was short, and soon, they were back in breezy coastal North Carolina. Brody stopped on the steps outside the airport doors and gazed up. He blinked against the bright-blue sky laced with big fluffy white clouds. "Happy clouds?" He jutted his chin upward.

Storm nodded. "Happy clouds."

Brody grinned at her smile and realized he was happy, too. He curled his arm around her waist. "I'm driving us back home, sweetheart."

She giggled but let him lead. As he drove them back to town, he felt her reach across the console and catch his hand in hers. The warmth of her skin took his breath away. He smiled as she gave him a gentle squeeze. Soon, they crossed the drawbridge into Sweetwater Harbor, and they stopped at Muriel and Cordell's house, where a variety of vehicles lined the sandy yard.

Storm made the rounds, greeting family like she had not seen them in years.

Winter had beaten them to town by a mere hour, and Brody was instantly impressed with the man. While not an identical copy of Storm, Winter clearly was her twin.

Winter Gallagher had that same red-blond hair, with his short military crop hiding his natural wave. They shared the same complexion, freckles, changeable blue-green eyes, and many of the same facial features. Winter stood several inches taller over Storm, and he clearly carried a soldier's physique and wore a warrior's wariness.

As parents and siblings cried and carried on, Brody sought out Calder. Gathered with his friend in a quiet corner, he heaved a weary sigh and leaned against the wall.

"You look like you've been through hell, buddy," Calder observed, concern lighting his eyes. "Was she that rough? You've barely been gone three days."

Brody grinned. "You won't believe the stuff I've seen. I tell you, Calder, I feel like I've been struck by a truck. But I've never felt more alive."

Calder smiled. "Well, it's good to have you back. And I bet whatever happened out there was good for you." He paused, resting his hand on Brody's shoulder. "Are you ready to stand up for me the day after tomorrow? Tonight, you and I are taking Winter out and treating him to dinner. How about What If?"

Brody looked over to where Winter was spinning Storm around in a circle, balancing her high over his head as she squealed in glee.

River and Raine rolled their eyes, poking each other.

Their parents watched, looking on with love and

tolerance for their grown brood.

How soon would little ones join the group? He cut a look over to Calder. It would be soon if he knew his friend.

The Gallagher clan was nosy, and noisy as a group, but the love they shared ran deep. He reflected over the things he'd experienced in the last few days and realized they also had something he'd never had before. Suddenly, he knew Calder was one heck of a lucky guy. He huffed another sigh, this one full of more longing than simply tired. "Sounds good, Calder." He was referring not only to being best man at the wedding but joining the family.

Raine walked over to where they stood. "I wanted to mention something in case it means anything special to you two. I ran into Joseph and Hazel Wickmore, the owners of the Golden Anchor Inn, and they told me they just had new guests check in."

Calder set his drink down. "It's an inn, Raine. They doubtlessly have new guests check in and out all the time."

Raine frowned at Calder and turned her attention to Brody. "They thought the men seemed shady. Hazel had asked if they were in town for the wedding, but they didn't seem to know what wedding she was referring to."

Calder shrugged and picked up his drink again. "I suppose people can come to town without it being for our wedding. Maybe they're just passing through. They could be traveling for business."

"Joseph said they didn't have much luggage, and they paid cash for two nights." Raine lowered her voice to almost a whisper. "Even the names they signed in with looked fake. John Smith?"

Brody felt his breath hitch. While his partner was willing to discount Raine's report, he wasn't so sure. He glanced at Storm and noticed the same look of concern. How should they handle this?

Calder laughed. "Lots of people are called John Smith, and it's their real name. I think you and the Wickmores are making more of this than there is." He rested a hand on Raine's shoulder. "Thanks for the gossip, but I'm sure these guys are legit."

Raine huffed. "But Calder—"

"But Raine!" Calder repeated with an exaggerated cry.

"Do you two want me to flip a coin to see who wins?" Brody reached into his pocket for a quarter. He hoped his light-hearted approach would defuse their heated conversation and increasing concerns. He brought a quarter out, and from the corner of his eye, he caught a swirl of fabric falling to the floor.

Calder's gaze followed it, too, rounded as realization dawned, and he turned to Brody, humor twitching his lips. "Planning on growing your hair out, pal?"

Heat flamed through Brody's cheeks. He bent to retrieve Storm's ponytail holder, cursing himself for not returning it. He ignored Raine's inhale of surprise and instead focused on Calder. "If I have to listen to you bickering any longer, I'll have no choice but to grow my hair long."

"Right."

Brody feigned nonchalance and thanked Raine for her research but agreed with Calder, then rushed to shepherd Storm away from the family. He led her outside, and once he was satisfied they were alone, he relayed Raine's comments.

She blanched.

She had pulled away from his steering grip, but as he spoke, he felt her fingers curl around his arm.

Despite the danger, he felt a stab of joy that his wild, tough, and independent Storm held to him in a fearful moment. Even if she probably didn't realize it. He did.

Brody's heart plunged to his stomach as he met and held Storm's gaze. Her lips parted ever so slightly. He could imagine her heart rate just spiked like his did. They found her.

"What are you going to do?"

"Shh! Not so loud."

"Fine." Brody fought to keep impatience out of his voice. "What are your plans?"

Storm placed a hand on his chest.

He was sorry to feel it leave his arm. He counted to five to keep from cradling her fingers in his palm. She had to be as scared as him, except she wouldn't show it. For a moment, his heart stung, and he wished she would let herself loose long enough to show her true feelings, even for a few moments.

They stood on the back porch, stealing what few minutes they could before someone came searching. Sea birds called and each scream grated on Brody's strung-out nerves.

"For now, I'm not doing anything."

He felt his jaw drop in shock. She was impossible! "But—"

She wagged her head. "I know you want to have at least half a dozen plans in place, but I can't roll that way. For now, until we know more about these guys, we won't do anything that will attract special attention. Think covert." She grinned and tapped her skull. "Take Winter for dinner like you guys planned. I'll meet with River and Raine as we planned. And we will see what unfolds next. Raine is fantastic at snooping around and getting private information."

He bit the inside of his lip, watching her eyes. Her words had some merit, but he wasn't one to sit back and impassively wait for things to happen. Not without…half a dozen plans in place. He moaned and squeezed his eyes shut. She was killing him. "Okay. Fine." He ground out the words like a tooth being pulled. "But, Storm Diana, I swear, I want to keep you within sight." Not only did he want her close by because of the possible danger of these unknown visitors, but he genuinely felt better when she was within eye and ear shot. Like his world was suddenly complete somehow only when she was around.

She smiled as she shook her head. Her fingers slowly inched up his chest.

His skin responded with warm shivers, keenly aware of her touch even through his thick sweater.

"Not possible, Brody, sorry. But I'll be with my sisters. We'll be okay."

He wasn't so sure.

The owners and staff of What If? rolled out the red carpet for Winter. People welcomed him home, and to the restaurant, like a long-lost favorite son. Or royalty. Brody, Calder, and Winter were ushered to a large corner table, one that afforded prime views of the overheard television screens playing various ball games. Frothy draft beers came in cold mugs, with a pitcher set in the middle for constant refills.

"Holy cow, wings and onion rings, too." Brody was taken aback as the server brought platters of appetizers without asking.

"They remember my favorites," Winter explained after he thanked the staff. He picked up an onion ring and poised it over the cup of dipping sauce. He grinned at Brody and Calder. "This all feels both humbling and surreal."

Brody agreed with the surreal part. He could not remember a time or a place where he experienced the royal treatment that he was a party to now.

Winter savored the onion ring, then took a long drink of beer, seemingly enjoying that even more. Finished, he wiped the foam off his lip and studied both Calder and Brody in turn. Then he blew out a breath. "Now, as I understand it, somehow both of you ended up without your clothes because of my sisters. How did that happen?"

"My situation wasn't so much River's fault." Calder explained how he ended up banned from his house and car, and subsequently, his luggage, when his father was murdered, and Muriel borrowed from Winter's closet to tide him over.

Brody snorted. "Storm tried to drown me in the ocean. Your mom insisted I needed to change to dry clothes."

Winter nodded and dipped a chicken wing into the sauce. "Storm. She's something else. Why'd she try drowning you?"

Brody faltered. Why indeed? He replayed their conversation over in his mind, seeking a concise reason.

Calder coughed, hiding his amusement behind a

wing dripping in ranch dressing.

Winter waited with one eyebrow raised.

"I'm really not sure," Brody finally confessed.

Winter grinned, his smile a mirror image of Storm's wicked amusement. "In that case, it might have been anything. She loves to pull the pin on any grenade."

While true, Brody thought it more accurate to say Storm knew how to turn any moment into a memory. Heaven knew he had plenty floating around inside his head.

"Your dad has said that a couple of times. He refers to her as testy."

Winter chuckled. "Maybe a little bit."

Whatever Cordell and Winter considered Storm, Brody knew he'd never forget the strong impressions she left stamped in his memory.

Now, what was he going to do about them when the wedding was upon them and his life in Atlanta awaited him? As did her dangerous data?

Chapter Sixteen

With only a day before the wedding, River and Calder were tied in knots.

Storm was sure they were determined to keep everyone else knotted like pretzels, too. She and River were sequestered away in Storm's room, going over the dress and accessories list one more time. They counted gowns, shoes, jewelry, and more, then matched them to the inventory list.

"I swear I had my shoes in the same bag as the hosiery." River pawed through the box the size of two regular shoeboxes, rattling tissue paper. "What happened to my shoes?"

"You could always walk the aisle barefoot."

River looked up from the search, rested her hands on her hips, and glared. "Is that supposed to be funny?"

Storm shrugged. She thought it was, and not altogether, a bad idea. She pulled another big shoebox to her and sorted through it. She held out the two pairs of shoes. "Look what I found."

River gasped and snatched the pair from her grip, inspecting them carefully.

"Geez, River, calm down. You act like you're going to the moon or something. You're just getting married."

River blew out a breath, returning her shoes to the correct shoebox. "I think going to the moon would be easier."

"You make a ceremony as easy or as complicated as you want. So relax and believe everything will work out okay."

"Easy for you to say, sister dear. You're not the one everyone will be staring at tomorrow."

Storm smirked. "Like people don't stare at you all the time already?"

"Ungrateful brat." River looked around and flung her well-worn wedding planner at Storm.

She deftly caught it. "I should burn this."

"Don't you dare!" River lunged for the planner.

Storm held it high in the air, laughing. "The wedding is tomorrow. What is possibly left to plan?"

"That also holds important phone numbers and emails. I can't lose that." River held her arm out, fingers wiggling in Storm's direction. "Hand it over."

"Here." Storm thrust it into River's palm.

"Why don't you go help the guys?" River cradled the book to her chest. "Or see if Raine needs help in town with the cake or catering?"

That Raine needed help was highly unlikely. A more dependable and capable soul was never born. But checking in with the guys was a break away from Reactive River and her crazy pre-wedding anxiety. "Not a bad idea, sis. See you later." Before she could be called back for more inventory stuff, Storm sprinted down the stairs and out the door.

The guys—Calder, Brody, and Winter—stood around Calder's car. Although the car was already spotless, they still buffed and shined the interior and exterior like they were polishing a rare diamond. Were they following River's orders to ensure the car shone like all her normal bling, or were they burning excess energy? She slipped up behind Winter and covered his eyes with her palms. "Guess who?"

"Umm, let's see." Winter brushed his hands over hers.

She felt the corners of his mouth pull up into a big smile. This was an old game they played.

"Ahh, it's the girl of my dreams."

About to offer a snappy comeback, Storm caught Brody's gaze over the car's hood. If she were to sum his expression up in two words, she'd label them— longing and envious. Her mind faltered as she registered his face and the possible meanings. She slipped her hands from Winter, aware he was waiting for her to continue the game.

"Storm?" Winter asked when she stood frozen.

"Yes. Um, yes, you're right. I'm the girl…" Her words trailed off.

Because she couldn't think and almost couldn't breathe. She was lost in Brody's angst and desire.

Slowly, the other guys noticed it, too.

Did they feel the electricity bouncing around them like a lightning storm? Or had time just stopped?

Calder recovered the fastest and cleared his throat. "Hey, um, Storm. We were just saying we needed more polish. You know, to, um, polish the car. We were going to send Brody down to the general store, but I'm worried he might get lost. Could you go with him?" He jerked a thumb at Brody.

Brody's head snapped from her to Calder. "What? Huh?" He blinked. "Oh, yeah, right. Polish. What do you say? Come along and keep me from getting lost?" He waved a few fingers in invitation.

She could spot a setup a mile away, and this one clearly was an impromptu setup. But she adored Calder for getting them together, regardless of the insane reason. She nodded at Brody and huffed an exaggerated sigh. "Someone needs to keep you safe. I guess."

They made it to the end of the drive before they burst into peals of laughter.

"Well, that was a surprise." Storm giggled.

"Um hum. Calder is the king of smooth."

She chuckled. "Let's walk. It's nice, and it will take us that much longer to get back. If the guys can wait to get the polish."

He took her hand in his, and his jaw jutted out. "They can wait."

"Good. Because I am in no hurry to return." She smiled over at him. "This is much better."

"Agreed." He looked around as they neared the intersection and turned toward town. "To be honest, I'm always happy to be in your company, but especially now with those new guys in town."

Storm frowned. "They can rip the town apart, ask questions of everyone they see, dig until the fishermen sail back in, and whatever else they want to do, they will not find that data."

"It's not the data I'm so worried about right now. It's you—" He paused, stopping his words and his steps. He took both of her hands in hers and searched her eyes. "It's your safety and that of everyone else in town. You pointed out these guys are not to be messed with."

His admission touched her heart, and she blinked back tears. "What would you do if they tried something? They are most likely armed…and determined." Not to mention very persistent.

Brody shook his head. "I don't know. I do know you face danger all the time, weather dangers. But I can't just leave you to face this alone. I need to be with you on this."

Hot tears burned her eyes. She sniffed once and nodded. "We'll leave town once it's safe, get the data delivered, and be home free. In the meantime, let's just act natural." She tugged him toward town.

They entered Tattinger's General Store, and Brody paused, looking around.

Storm wondered if he was looking for troublesome strangers or just taking in the store's eclectic vibe. She'd been in dozens of multipurpose stores, but Tattinger's was indeed unique. She tried looking at the worn wood floors that squeaked, the shelves laden with just about everything imaginable, and the rich smell of polished wood through his senses. Here, it was support local or do without.

"Hello, Storm, what can I do for you two?" Teddy Tattinger, Sr. came from the back room, rubbed his hands together. "You need anything for the wedding?"

"No, River has that all in hand. We need a can of car polish. For Calder's car."

"Of course. Our car products, washes, polishes, and the like, are all along that lower shelf." Tattinger pointed to a shelf along a long wall.

Brody guided her over and studied the wares while Teddy Sr. struck up a conversation about the events of tomorrow.

Seemed the whole town was excited about the wedding. Listening to him gush now, she found it hard to believe it almost didn't happen.

Brody selected a can of car polish.

She took it, handing it over to Teddy Sr.

He rang it up on a genuine old-fashioned cash register, complete with clicks, chirps, and a final bell.

She handed over a ten-dollar bill from her pocket.

He made change. He slid the can into a small paper sack and handed it over to Brody.

"Well, I guess that's mission accomplished," Storm said once they were back outside.

"Yes, but now we have an extra can of polish."

Storm shrugged. "They can consider it a wedding gift from me." She leaned a shoulder against his for a moment. "To be honest, I'm just glad we made it into town and haven't run into those guys Raine was talking about earlier. Mr. Smith and Mr. Smith from the Golden Anchor Inn."

"I agree."

Storm shook her head. "I don't know what I'd do if I see them again. I just want to get this all behind me."

"Me, too, honey." Brody reached for Storm's hand, liking how firm and warm it felt when they touched. "After all the grief Calder caused me since I got to town, he should give me the gift."

Storm slowed down, jerking his arm back.

Brody turned back, realizing he might have opened his mouth and inserted both his feet about the time he noticed her narrowed eyes.

"What do you mean by that, McGee?" She completely yanked free of his grip and her voice dropped an octave.

Oh-oh. He thought fast, if only he could find one. His mind was utterly blank. "What do I mean?" he repeated. "I mean—"

"I knew it! You came to town to stop the wedding!"

Brody stepped back, dropped the bag, and raised his arms, ready to defend himself.

A couple of people strolled by, glanced their way, and kept on walking.

Whether they wanted to avoid her temper or honestly had no interest in other's business, he didn't know. "Can you calm down so I can explain what I meant?" Like he had any idea how to do that. He would probably need dynamite to change her mind now.

Her nostrils flared.

The gesture reminded Brody of the wild mares that walked the shoreline and grassy spaces.

She shook her head, red hair billowing around her. "No, I don't think so. There's no need to walk me farther, because I know the way home. And likewise, Mr. McGee, you should know the way back to Atlanta." She took a step toward him, finger raised to his chest. "I will not have you destroy their wedding."

He intercepted her finger one moment before she punched him in the chest.

She huffed once and spun, striding away.

Now what? He wasn't prepared for another round of her attitude, but he sure wasn't leaving town, either. Not until Calder was married and he accompanied Storm to hand over her data, whether she liked it or not.

He blew out a frustrated breath and watched her backside sway as she marched along the street. Doubtlessly, alarms would go off when she returned without him. Calder would come looking for him. At times like this, he wondered why he didn't just grab Calder and throw him into the car when he first came to town like his original plan had been.

But then he'd have missed meeting Storm Diana. And meeting her was worth just about anything. If only he could calm her ferocious temper a little. He exhaled again, looked around for any witnesses to their altercation, and to search for divine inspiration. His gaze caught on someone, and his blood chilled. *Oh no…*

He rushed up to Storm, grabbed her by the upper arm, and spun her around. Without giving her a chance to fight him, he pressed her against the brick wall next to them.

She tried to scream.

But he plastered his mouth over hers, muffling her protests. Tropical scents of coconut and jasmine flooded his nostrils. He captured her hands as she started to flail him and placed them on his butt, firmly holding them in place.

Her nails clawed through the fabric of his khakis. She tried to bring her knee up.

He pressed his weight against her, wedging her into the wall and holding her nearly immobile. He was smart enough not to force his tongue into her mouth, lest she bite it off. She tried to chew his lip, and he latched onto her bottom lip. The more he held her, the angrier she became. Her muscles strained against him, while his ached with the battle. He faced the fury in her eyes and held on. His beautiful wild mare was fighting for all she was worth.

Finally, he could hold her no longer. His chest burned with the effort she required. He released her and stepped back, breathless, and shaky with exertion.

"What in the world are—"

"If you'll settle down one second, I can explain," he hissed, leaning closer but keeping a respectful distance should he have to retreat. "There." He cupped her chin and turned her head toward the backs of the two men. "I just repaid the favor."

Storm looked at the retreating men, then back at Brody. She inhaled sharply, turned back, her jaw slack and eyes wide. "Oh no."

He felt her sag against him. A shiver rolled over her, and he recognized the depth of her concern. "That's not quite what I said, but close enough."

"I didn't want to believe Raine they were here. How'd they track me to Sweetwater Harbor?"

"I don't know, but they really are here." He sympathized. She was probably beginning to think she'd never be safe. He pulled her into his arms, offering a hug, while keeping an eye on the street, to ensure they didn't come back. Or to be ready if they did. He swallowed, wanting to avoid a confrontation at all costs. He patted her back. "We need to get back to the house, without them seeing us."

"What, no plan, Brody?" She shot him a Cheshire grin.

"Nope. Not this time." Despite his concern, he admired her sass. "This isn't something I normally have to think about."

She nibbled her bottom lip, her gaze straying in the men's direction. "I could call Raine or Mom and have her come pick us up in their car."

He considered that, tilting his head to one side. Then, spotting the obvious, he smiled. "How would you explain why we suddenly couldn't walk back?"

She grinned. "I'd say you were too tired and

needed a lift."

Of course, she would. "Maybe we could go inside one of the restaurants. We could always hide behind menus if they come in." Although another passionate kiss sounded good. He couldn't think of a better way to die than kissing Storm.

No, on second thought, she would never jeopardize any of the people in town. He had no idea what these guys would do if they found her, but she would not put anyone in danger. He allowed himself a grin. For a woman who thrived on adrenaline and excitement she would not subject her friends or family to a serious threat.

"What's so funny, McGee?" Without waiting, she plowed ahead. "I don't think going back home is wise. We need to get out of town for a little while."

"The wedding is tomorrow. Big dinner tonight, remember?"

"How can we attend the rehearsal dinner with those goons on the loose?"

The mixture of fury and worry on her face cracked Brody's heart. He squeezed her softly. "If they come back, and they try threatening anyone in your family, or here in town, they will have to deal with the two of us." He hoped he sounded braver than he felt. Her tiny smile fueled him. "Right now, we need to calm down and make an action plan."

She nodded and blinked her teary eyes.

He brushed the gathering moisture away with his thumbs. His brain failed to think up a single way to protect her, but as he felt her slight quiver and the wetness of her tears between his fingers, he vowed he'd do anything for her. Anything. And everything.

****

"Just as a gem cannot be polished without friction, no person can be perfected without trials," Storm said absently, gaze drifting to the route the men had gone.

"What?" Brody asked, brows wrinkling. He shook his head.

She smiled. "Something my daddy sometimes says. I suppose this is one of those trials."

He traced a knuckle down her cheek, making her involuntarily shiver. His gaze was tender. "I think you're already perfect."

Storm could have melted on the spot, like the humidity that spiked after a summer rainstorm, had it not been for the seriousness of the goons creeping through her town. She blinked back the moisture in her eyes caused by Brody's soft touch and softer words. No time to be carried away on a cloud. "Okay, here's what we can do. We can go to the marina or get on River's boat, *The Sea Quest,* and go out on the water. We'll be safe there."

He smiled softly, his knuckle still resting against her throat. "For how long? Are we to stay indefinitely on the boat?"

Good point. Darn, she was clueless about what to do. Why hadn't she considered this possibility when they tracked her to the airport? She could kick herself for letting her guard down. The contacts at the government counted on her to be careful.

"Whoa, Storm. Reel in whatever thoughts are clouding your mind." Brody rested his hands on her shoulders, as if to steady her. His gaze sought hers. "This will be okay. We'll work through this together." He smiled.

She wanted to lean into him so badly. Instead, she forced herself to stand straight and meet him in the eye. "So what do you have in mind?" Heaven knew she was coming up blank.

"I'm thinking those bozos don't have a clear description of what you look like. They've passed you twice already and didn't give you a second glance. And they are not expecting you to be with a handsome dude such as myself." He sent her a flirty wink. "So, let's work this to our advantage. We go to your parents' and hang out there for the rehearsal dinner and through the wedding. We blend in as much as possible, and as soon as we can, we leave town with your research and get it delivered. Problem solved."

Storm exhaled a heavy breath. For once, having someone come alongside and help solve a problem felt good. She nodded, smiled her gratitude, and reached for his hands. "Let's take the beach route back home. Hopefully, they won't be walking along the beach looking for me."

He grinned, flashing Storm a hint of twin dimples. "If they are, I can lay you down on the sand and repay the favor again."

She trailed a fingertip along his jaw, waiting as he inhaled sharply, eyes darkened, and body grew taut. She uttered a guttural purr and partially closed her eyes. "That would be fine by me whether we see them or not. In fact, I think you owe me interest."

Chapter Seventeen

Calder stood at the altar, adjusting the bowtie on his velvet tuxedo.

Brody reached out, slapping his hand away. "Stop that," he admonished. "You look fine."

Calder scowled. "Are they ever getting here?"

At the anxiety in his friend's voice, Brody chuckled. "In due time, buddy. Girls like those will get here when they are good and ready."

And nothing was as ready as the chapel. Though small, the room was tastefully decorated with sparkling colors of tan and aqua from the towering florals at the altar and entrance, to the delicate pew ornaments, and finally to the shimmery boutonnieres each man wore. Nothing had escaped River's shine. *If* she and her entourage ever arrived. Poor Calder was going to stroke out.

"Amen," Winter echoed softly.

His expression a perfect example of a soldier's solemn expectation, however nothing could erase the happiness in his eye. He and Brody acted as Calder's best men. The male Gallagher cousins served as ushers.

The music began. Miss Daphne, the schoolteacher and River's secretary, was also the church's designated organist. *Small towns.* They were something. The doors opened. Raine and Storm, River's bridesmaids, entered, slowly sauntering up the aisle and both wearing big smiles, shimmery beige gowns, and strappy heels.

Brody's heart slammed to a painful halt, then jerked forward as Storm neared, her smile beaming solely upon him. Her blue-green gaze fixed on his as she sashayed closer, clutching the small bouquet of aqua roses. He felt his jaw drop.

He had carefully analyzed all the experiences from his time out in the field with the storm-chasing team, and his thoughts and feelings since returning, including their narrow escape from the thugs who were searching for her. And he arrived at one startling conclusion: a person could be happy almost anywhere, doing almost anything, just as long as they were with the one person they loved. Lasting love was a complex emotion that required energy and time to maintain. The truth was one he suspected Calder had already learned with River. Further, he determined the view was wonderful to be had, and shared, if he was following Storm.

He even figured he could get used to going on chases with Storm, once he conquered his fear of nature's wilder—and deadlier—side. Some perks were possible to storm chasing with Storm. Like the adrenaline rush, a natural high. Like seeing Storm shine like a diamond in her natural element. And looking at her resembling an angel reflected in a police car's blue halo of light.

Brody drew in a deep breath, held it, and then slowly let it out. Yeah, he could do this.

More cousins followed and filled in behind Storm and Raine. Brody barely remembered their names when he was introduced yesterday. Autumn, Spring, Honor, Harmony, and he already forgot the names of the rest.

Wagner's "Lohengrin March" began, and everyone

stood straighter, all gazes in the small chapel swiveling to the doors in eager expectation as "Here Comes the Bride" echoed through the room.

Cordell Gallagher entered, River on his arm, slowly marching her down the aisle. Her wispy white veil barely covered her happy smile. The white dress shimmered and shone with countless bows, rows and ruffles of sparkles, sequins, and bling. Diamonds glinted from her ears and at her throat. If the roof were open, her radiating shine could be seen from passing airplanes.

Halting before Calder, Cordell released her, pausing to lift her veil and give her a cheek kiss. "I love you, honey," he whispered before winking at Calder and moving to join Muriel on the front bench.

River handed her bouquet to Storm and joined hands with Calder, their gazes locked only on each other.

Brody kept peeking over at Storm, his heart racing as she glanced back, that impish little smile getting under his skin. What was she thinking?

The minister cleared his throat.

Brody looked back at him, heat warming his neck. He could almost hear Storm's soft giggle.

"Dearly beloved," the minister began, "we are gathered here today…"

****

River stood on the chair, eyes closed as she tossed the bouquet over her shoulder amid shouts of women.

"I got it!" Storm cried as she stretched out, leaning forward to catch the flowers. A wild thrill raced over her as the petals and ribbons landed as neatly into her palms as a baseball. She held it to her nose, breathing deep as the other ladies in the circle moaned and drifted away.

"Bet you catch a mean fly ball, too," Brody commented, walking up.

"I can." She clutched the bouquet to her chest, suddenly feeling out of breath. And suddenly very warm. He looked so good in a tux. He smelled good. She breathed in his spicy cologne.

The family and friends surrounding them quietly slipped away, leaving them as the only two people in the room.

"That was some ceremony." Brody took another step closer.

She could see his heavy breathing, and she felt her breath escape her, too. "It was beautiful."

"Raine outdid herself on the cake."

Storm nodded. "It is towering and lavish. She worked hard on it."

"It showed." He leaned close.

His hushed words fanned her warmed cheeks with wintergreen scent from his gum.

"We dodged those guys, and I think we'll be okay to slip out of town tomorrow."

She blinked, bringing her attention from how sexy he looked and smelled and back to the matter at hand. "I already called my contact and told them to expect us tomorrow late afternoon. We should leave about six thirty."

"I'll be ready, with coffee for the road. You know, that was only the second wedding I've even attended."

That surprised her. "I would have thought you'd been invited to several weddings by now."

He grinned. "Oh, I've been invited to a bunch. I've

only just attended one other."

Interesting. She licked her lips, feeling heat filling her cheeks and spreading. His direct stare was working. She wondered what lay behind that stare and how best to find out.

Suddenly he gripped her hands in his. "Storm Diana." He paused to clear his throat. "Storm, I, uh…" He quickly dropped to one knee and smiled awkwardly. "Oops. Okay, proposal take two. Storm, wherever in the world you happen to be, whether it be cozy Sweetwater Harbor or the far reaches of disaster zones or somewhere between, I want to be alongside you. I want to learn about and share all the facets of love with you. I want to eat peanut butter cookies on satin sheets with you."

She covered her mouth with the palm of a hand as surprise rolled over her. Her chest filled with emotion. She felt like someone tightened a belt around her ribs too tight. She couldn't draw a breath.

She was being proposed to? Hadn't she always assumed she'd remain single?

And Brody…he was so opposite of her—with his plans and logic and safe ways. But he'd ridden out the storm with her and never complained. He'd stepped into her world and met her there.

Her breath burned inside her, and the room tilted. Sweat dripped down her back. *Marriage?*

No. Was he serious?

He stared, concern puckering his brows. Was he afraid she would say no?

For a fraction of a second, she considered just that. *No* would be the safe way to handle this…and also the saddest way. Somewhere in the storm and their time in town, she'd fallen in love.

He started to raise a hand, reaching for her. If he touched her, she'd shatter like glass. She closed her eyes and inhaled. He loved her. She breathed in again…deeper. She was both scared and exhilarated. Cold and hot. Afraid and excited.

"Storm?"

She heard him whisper her name, a worried rasp. She stared at their joined hands. No one ever made her feel so alive inside, so desired, or so perfect before Brody. Was there any other answer to give him?

For a moment, her mind flickered back to the time she and River sat in her room, talking about places to get married. Storm had tried to envision where she would select. At the time, the idea seemed like sheer folly. Now, she quickly reran the list of places through her mind.

Fireworks. She wanted a big celebration. She didn't care for the planned details. Plans weren't her thing. But she wanted fireworks at the end. Bombs of color lighting the night sky. She wanted the ceremony to be epic and unforgettable. In a wide-open space, with the sky as a ceiling and the ground as a carpet and the weather for music. And fireworks for decorations.

"Storm?"

The desperation in his voice rattled her.

Without thinking any longer, she plunged ahead, nodding up and down rapidly as hot tears filled her eyes. Her grip tightened on his hands. "Brody McGee, I know some things a man ought to know. One is to recognize true love, and once you find it, you hold on tight with both hands and never let it go." She paused. "But do you know how to be a husband?"

He blushed, then grinned. "I've never been one, but I think I can learn. If you can learn to be a wife." He lifted an eyebrow. "What do you say?"

"I will learn to be a wife." She sniffed, tears welling in her eyes. "You probably don't know how you cause good shivers all over my body. It's crazy how you affect me. I think I have to marry you. And I'd be honored to marry you." She laughed and gripped his hands. "Yes, let's do this!"

As far as proposals and acceptances went, theirs might be considered unusual; however it worked for them. Storm never envisioned herself getting married, but now, she could not picture her life without Brody in it every day. Chasing storms together or walking the beach of town, or whatever she was doing, he had to be a part of it. She squealed as he drew her into a warm hug. Storm never felt happier than looking into the eyes of the man she loved.

"One thing, though," she whispered.

"Anything."

"You plan this thing. Do a Plan B, C, and D, if you want. River has a planner full of names you can contact. Date, time, location, guest list, and stuff doesn't matter to me. Raine can do the cake and food. Otherwise, all I want is an outside location and fireworks. Big, colorful, loud popping fireworks." He gave her a raised-eyebrow look, which soon changed to a wide smile. He rested his forehead against hers, his breath warm on her cheeks.

"I'll plan the best wedding possible, and I promise you will have fireworks as wild and wonderful as you, my love."

Epilogue

Raine turned the *Closed* sign, turned off the lights, and exited Sweet Obsessions. What a whirlwind month it had been. She tested the lock of her bakery and started down the street. She was due to meet River and Calder for dinner soon.

As she walked down the street, she replayed the last few weeks. First, she had quite possibly outdone herself with the wedding cake. Though requests continued to pour in for various cakes, topping their creation was going to be hard. People were still talking about it.

She let out a long breath. River and Calder were married. *Finally*. River could stop driving everyone crazy with planning every single detail. And now Storm and Brody were engaged. For as much as they argued at first, they turned on the heat quick enough.

Raine laughed, the happy sound going out into the salty air. If the decision was up to Storm, they'd run off one day and come back married. Brody was insisting on a long engagement, with every detail planned. Maybe River would give him a good deal on a used wedding planner. She chuckled again.

Plus, she had more materials to use for her continuing garden project—thanks to her last trip to Lady Beth and The Silk Road store.

Brody and Calder both planned to stay in town.

Life, as far as she could tell, was both fulfilling and satisfying. Now who could ask for more?

She neared the corner, then she spotted a dark-haired man behind the wheel of the seafoam-colored, classic muscle car. His stare met hers, and they simultaneously locked.

He slowed the car.

She hesitated, nearly coming to a full stop. A light sweat broke out over her. *Wow! Just wow.* Who was he? And what was he doing in Sweetwater Harbor?

A word about the author…

Ryan Jo Summers lives in Western North Carolina where she draws inspiration for her fiction stories. She has had over a dozen fiction novels, novellas or anthology inclusions published since 2012. Several of her previous works have been nominated by industry and peer reviewed awards. She also writes non-fiction articles and essays for local, regional, and national magazines, devotionals, and trade journals. She enjoys cooking, gardening, reading, painting, and enjoying birds and nature, or simply gathering with friends. She is an animal advocate and likes to foster unwanted pets for area rescue organizations.

http://www.ryanjosummers.com

Other Titles by This Author

Blue Moon and Starry Skies

River's Journey, Winds of Destiny #1

Snickerdoodle Surprise